BE CAREFUL WHAT YOU WISH FOR

GOOSEBUMPS®
Also available as ebooks

Goosebumps®

BE CAREFUL WHAT YOU WISH FOR

R.L. STINE

SCHOLASTIC INC.

NEW YORK TORONTO LONDON AUCKLAND
SYDNEY MEXICO CITY NEW DELHI HONG KONG

ISBN 978-0-545-03524-8

Goosebumps book series created by Parachute Press, Inc.

Copyright © 1993 by Scholastic Inc.

All rights reserved. Published by Scholastic Inc., *Publishers since 1920.* SCHOLASTIC, GOOSEBUMPS, GOOSEBUMPS HORRORLAND, and associated logos are trademarks and/or registered trademarks of Scholastic Inc.

28 27 26 25   18   19/0

Printed in the U.S.A.   40
First printing, February 2009

"Behind the Screams" bonus material by Matthew D. Payne

1

Judith Bellwood deliberately tripped me in math class.

I saw her white sneaker shoot out into the aisle. Too late.

I was carrying my notebook up to the chalkboard to put a problem on the board. My eyes were on the scrawls in my notebook. I'm not the neatest writer in the world.

And before I could stop, I saw the white sneaker shoot out. I tripped over it and went sprawling to the floor, landing hard on my elbows and knees. Of course all the papers flew out of my notebook and scattered everywhere.

And the whole class thought it was a riot. Everyone was laughing and cheering as I struggled to pull myself up. Judith and her pal Anna Frost laughed hardest of all.

I landed on my funny bone, and the pain vibrated up and down my whole body. As I climbed to my feet and then bent to pick up my notebook papers, I knew my face was as red as a tomato.

"Nice move, Sam!" Anna called, a big grin on her face.

"Instant replay!" someone else shouted.

I glanced up to see a triumphant glow in Judith's green eyes.

I'm the tallest girl in my seventh-grade class. No. Correct that. I'm the tallest *kid* in my seventh-grade class. I'm at least two inches taller than my friend Cory Blinn, and he's the tallest guy.

I'm also the biggest klutz who ever stumbled over the face of the earth. I mean, just because I'm tall and slender doesn't mean I have to be graceful. And believe me, I'm not.

But why is it such a riot when I stumble over a wastebasket or drop my tray in the lunchroom or trip over someone's foot in math class?

Judith and Anna are just cruel, that's all.

I know they both call me Stork behind my back. Cory told me they do.

And Judith is always making fun of my name, which is Byrd. Samantha Byrd. *"Why don't you fly away, Byrd!"* That's what she's always saying to me. Then she and Anna laugh as if that's the funniest joke they've ever heard.

"Why don't you fly away, Byrd!"

Ha-ha. Big joke.

Cory says that Judith is just jealous of me. But that's stupid. I mean, why should Judith be jealous? She's not nine feet tall. She's about five-two, perfect for a twelve-year-old. She's graceful. She's athletic. And she's really pretty, with pale, creamy skin, big green eyes, and wavy copper-colored hair down to her shoulders.

So what's to be jealous about?

I think Cory is just trying to make me feel better — and doing a *lousy* job of it.

Anyway, I gathered all my papers together and shoved them back into the notebook. Sharon asked if I was okay. (Sharon is my math teacher. We call all the teachers by their first names here at Montrose Middle School.)

I muttered that I was fine, even though my elbow was throbbing like crazy. And I copied the problem on the board.

The chalk squeaked, and everyone groaned and complained. I can't help it. I've never been able to write on the board without squeaking the chalk.

It isn't *such* a big deal — *is* it?

I heard Judith whisper some crack about me to Anna, but I couldn't hear what it was. I glanced up from the problem to see the two of them snickering and smirking at me.

And wouldn't you know it — I couldn't solve the problem. I had something wrong with the equation, and I couldn't figure out what.

Sharon stepped up behind me, her skinny arms crossed over her ugly chartreuse sweater. She moved her lips as she read what I had written, trying to see where I had gone wrong.

And of course Judith raised her hand and called out, "I see the problem, Sharon. Byrd can't add. Four and two is six, not five."

I could feel myself blushing again.

Where would I be without Judith to point out my mistakes to the whole class?

Everyone was laughing again. Even Sharon thought it was funny.

And I had to stand there and take it. Good old Samantha, the class klutz. The class idiot.

My hand was shaking as I erased my stupid mistake and wrote in the right numbers.

I was *so angry*. At Judith. And at myself.

But I kept it together as I walked — carefully — back to my seat. I didn't even glance at Judith as I walked past her.

I kept it together until Home Ec. class that afternoon.

Then it got ugly.

Daphne is our teacher in Home Ec. I like Daphne. She is a big, jolly woman with several chins and a great sense of humor.

The rumor is that Daphne always makes us bake cakes and pies and brownies so that she can eat them all after we leave the class.

That's kind of mean, I think. But it's probably a little bit true.

We have Home Ec. right after lunch, so we're never very hungry. Most of what we make wouldn't make good *dog food*, anyway. So it mostly gets left in the Home Ec. room.

I always look forward to the class. Partly because Daphne is a fun teacher. And partly because it's the one class where there's no homework.

The only bad thing about Home Ec. class is that Judith is in it, too.

Judith and I had a little run-in in the lunchroom. I sat down at the far end of the table, as far away from her as I could get. But I still heard her telling a couple of eighth-graders, "Byrd tried to fly in math class."

Everyone laughed and stared at me.

"You tripped me, Judith!" I shouted angrily. My mouth was full of egg salad, which dribbled down my chin when I shouted.

And everyone laughed at me again.

Judith said something, which I couldn't hear over all the noise in the lunchroom. She smirked at me and tossed her red hair behind her shoulders.

I started to get up and go over to her. I don't know *what* I was thinking of doing. But I was so angry, I wasn't thinking too clearly.

Luckily, Cory appeared across the table. He dropped his lunch down on the table, turned the chair around backwards the way he always does, and sat down.

"What's four plus two?" he teased.

"Forty-two," I replied, rolling my eyes. "Do you *believe* Judith?" I asked bitterly.

"Of course I believe Judith," he said, pulling open his brown lunch bag. "Judith is Judith."

"What's that supposed to mean?" I snapped.

He shrugged. A grin broke out across his face. "I don't know."

Cory is kind of cute. He has dark brown eyes that sort of crinkle up in the corners, a nose that's a little too long, and a funny, crooked smile.

6

He has great hair, but he never brushes it. So he never takes off his cap. It's an Orlando Magic cap, even though he doesn't know or care about the team. He just likes the cap.

He peeked into his lunch bag and made a face.

"Again?" I asked, wiping egg salad off the front of my T-shirt with a napkin.

"Yeah. Again," he replied glumly. He pulled out the same lunch his father packed for him every single morning. A grilled cheese sandwich and an orange. "Yuck!"

"Why does your dad give you grilled cheese every day?" I asked. "Didn't you tell him it gets cold and slimy by lunchtime?"

"I told him," Cory groaned, picking up half of the sandwich in one hand and examining it as if it were some sort of science lab specimen. "He said it's good protein."

"How can it be good protein if you throw it in the trash every day?" I asked.

Cory grinned his crooked grin. "I didn't tell him that I throw it in the trash every day." He shoved the rubbery sandwich back into the bag and started to peel the orange.

"It's a good thing you came by," I said, swallowing the last bite of my egg salad sandwich. "I was about to get up and go murder Judith over there."

We both glanced down the table. Judith and the two eighth-graders had their chairs tilted back

7

and were laughing about something. One of the eighth-graders had a *People* magazine, I think, and she was showing a picture in it to the others.

"Don't murder Judith," Cory advised, still peeling the orange. "You'll get into trouble."

I laughed, scornful laughter. "You kidding? I'd get an award."

"If you murder Judith, your basketball team will never win another game," Cory said, concentrating on the orange.

"Ooh, that's cruel!" I exclaimed. I tossed my balled-up aluminum foil at him. It bounced off his chest and dropped to the floor.

He was right, of course. Judith was the best player on our team, the Montrose Mustangs. She was the *only* good player. She could dribble really well without getting the ball tangled up in her legs. And she had a great shooting eye.

I, of course, was the *worst* player on the team.

I admit it. I'm a total klutz, as I've said, which doesn't get you very far on the basketball court.

I really hadn't wanted to be on the Mustangs. I knew I'd stink.

But Ellen insisted. Ellen is the girls' basketball coach. Ellen insisted I be on the team.

"Sam, you're so tall!" she told me. "You've *got* to play basketball. You're a natural!"

Sure, I'm a natural. A natural klutz.

I can't shoot at all, not even foul shots. *Especially* not foul shots.

And I can't run without tripping over my own Reeboks. And my hands are small, even though the rest of me isn't, so I'm not too good at passing or catching the ball.

I think Ellen has learned her lesson: *Tall ain't all.*

But now she's too embarrassed to take me off the team. And I keep at it. I work hard at practice. I mean, I keep thinking I'll get better. I couldn't get any worse.

If only Judith wasn't such a hotshot.

And if only she was nicer to me.

But, as Cory put it, "Judith is Judith." She's always yelling at me during practice, and making fun of me, and making me feel two feet tall (which I sometimes wish I were)!

"Byrd, why don't you give us a break and fly away!"

If she says that one more time, I'll punch out her lights. I really will.

"What are you thinking about, Sam?" Cory's voice broke into my bitter thoughts.

"About Judith, of course," I muttered. "Miss Perfect."

"Hey, stop," he said, pulling apart the orange sections. "You have good qualities, too, you know."

"Oh, really?" I snapped. "What are my good qualities? That I'm tall?"

"No." He finally popped an orange section into his mouth. I never saw anyone take so long to eat an orange! "You're also smart," he said. "And you're funny."

"Thanks a bunch," I replied, frowning.

"And you're very generous," he added. "You're so generous, you're going to give me that bag of potato chips, right?" He pounced on it before I could grab it away from him.

I *knew* there was a reason for his compliments.

I watched Cory stuff down my potato chips. He didn't even offer me one.

Then the bell rang, and I hurried to Home Ec.

Where I totally lost it.

What happened was this: We were making tapioca pudding. And it was really messy.

We all had big orange mixing bowls, and the ingredients were spread out on the long table next to the stove.

I was busily stirring mine. It was nice and gloppy, and it made this great *glop glop* sound as I stirred it with a long wooden spoon.

My hands were sticky for some reason. I had probably spilled some of the pudding on them. So I stopped to wipe them on my apron.

I was being pretty neat — for me. There were only a few yellow puddles of pudding on my table. Most of it was actually in the mixing bowl.

I finished stirring and, when I looked up, there was Judith.

I was a little surprised because she had been working on the other side of the room by the windows. We generally keep as far apart from each other as possible.

Judith had this odd smile on her face. And as she approached me, she pretended to trip.

I *swear* she only pretended to trip!

And she spilled her whole mixing bowl of tapioca onto my shoes.

My brand-new blue Doc Martens.

"Oops!" she said.

That's all. Just "Oops!"

I looked down at my brand-new shoes covered in gloppy yellow pudding.

And that's when I lost it.

I uttered an angry roar and went for Judith's throat.

I didn't plan it or anything. I think it was temporary insanity.

I just reached out both hands and grabbed Judith by the throat, and began to strangle her.

I mean, they were *brand-new shoes*!

Judith started struggling and tried to scream. She pulled my hair and tried to scratch me.

But I held onto her throat and roared some more, like an angry tiger.

And Daphne had to pull us apart.

She pulled me away by the shoulders, then thrust her wide body between us, blocking our view of each other.

I was panting loudly. My chest was heaving up and down.

"Samantha! Samantha! What were you *doing*?" I *think* that's what Daphne was screaming.

I couldn't really hear her. I had this roaring in my ears, loud as a waterfall. I think it was just my anger.

Before I knew it, I had pushed myself away from the table and was running out of the room. I ran out into the empty hall — and stopped.

I didn't know what to do next. I was *so* angry.

If I had three wishes, I told myself, *I know what they would be: Destroy Judith! Destroy Judith! Destroy Judith!*

Little did I know that I would soon get my wish.

All three of them.

Daphne made Judith and me shake hands and apologize to each other after she dragged me back into the classroom. I had to do it. It was either that or be tossed out of school.

"It really was an accident," Judith muttered under her breath. "What's your problem, Byrd?"

Not much of an apology, if you ask me.

But I shook hands with her. I didn't need my parents being called to school because their daughter had tried to strangle a classmate.

And I showed up — reluctantly — for basketball practice after school. I knew if I didn't show, Judith would tell everyone that she had scared me away.

I showed up because I knew Judith didn't want me to. Which I think is as good a reason as any.

Also, I needed the exercise. I needed to run back and forth across the court a few hundred times to get the anger out. I needed to sweat out the frustration from not being able to finish strangling Judith.

"Let's do some fast laps," Ellen suggested.

Some of the other girls groaned, but I didn't. I started running before Ellen even blew her whistle.

We were all in shorts and sleeveless T-shirts. Ellen wore gray sweats that were baggy in all the wrong places. She had frizzy red hair, and she was so straight and skinny, she looked sort of like a kitchen match.

Ellen wasn't very athletic. She told us she coached girls' basketball because they paid her extra, and she needed the money.

After running our laps around the gym, practice went pretty much as usual.

Judith and Anna passed the ball to each other a lot. And they both took a lot of shots — jump shots, layups, even hook shots.

The others tried to keep up with them.

I tried not to be noticed.

I was still simmering about the tapioca pudding disaster and wanted as little contact with Judith — or *anyone* — as possible. I mean, I was really feeling glum.

And watching Judith sink a twenty-foot jumper, catch her own rebound, and scoop a perfect two-handed shovel pass to Anna wasn't helping to cheer me up one bit.

Of course, things got worse.

Anna actually passed the ball to me. I muffed it. It bounced off my hands, hit me in the forehead, and rolled away.

"Heads up, Byrd!" I heard Ellen cry.

I kept running. I tried not to look upset that I had blown my first opportunity of the practice.

A few minutes later, I saw the ball flying toward me again, and I heard Judith shout, "Get this one, Stork!"

I was so startled that she had called me Stork to my face that I *caught* the ball. I started to dribble to the basket — and Anna reached a hand in and easily stole the ball. She spun around and sent an arching shot to the basket, which nearly went in.

"Nice steal, Anna!" Ellen cried.

Breathing hard, I turned angrily to Judith. "What did you call me?"

Judith pretended she didn't hear me.

Ellen blew the whistle. "Fast breaks!" she shouted.

We practiced fast breaks three at a time. Dribbling fast, we'd pass the ball back and forth. Then the one under the hoop with the ball was supposed to take the shot.

I need to practice slow *breaks!* I thought to myself.

I had no trouble keeping up with the others. I mean, I had the longest legs, after all. I could run

15

fast enough. I just couldn't do anything else while I was running.

As Judith, Anna, and I came roaring down the court, I prayed I wouldn't make a total fool of myself. Sweat poured down my forehead. My heart was racing.

I took a short pass from Anna, dribbled under the basket, and took a shot. The ball flew straight up in the air, then bounced back to the floor. It didn't even come close to the backboard.

I could hear girls laughing on the sidelines. Judith and Anna had their usual superior smirks on their faces. "Good eye!" Judith called, and everyone laughed some more.

After twenty minutes of fast-break torture, Ellen blew her whistle. "Scrimmage," she called out. That was the signal for us to divide into two teams and play each other.

I sighed, wiping perspiration off my forehead with the back of my hand. I tried to get into the game. I concentrated hard, mainly on not messing up. But I was pretty discouraged.

Then, a few minutes into the game, Judith and I both dove for the ball at the same time.

Somehow, as I dove, my arms outstretched, Judith's knee came up hard — and plunged like a knife into my chest.

The pain shot through my entire body.

I tried to cry out. But I couldn't make a sound.

I uttered a weird gasping noise, sort of like the honk of a sick seal — and realized I couldn't breathe.

Everything turned red. Bright, shimmering red.

Then black.

I knew I was going to die.

Having your breath knocked out has to be the worst feeling in the world. It's just so scary. You try to breathe, and you can't. And the pain just keeps swelling, like a balloon being blown up right inside your chest.

I really thought I was dead meat.

Of course I was perfectly okay a few moments later. I still felt a little shaky, a little dizzy. But I was basically okay.

Ellen insisted that one of the girls walk me to the locker room. Naturally, Judith volunteered. As we walked, she apologized. She said it had been an accident. Totally an accident.

I didn't say anything. I didn't want her to apologize. I didn't want to talk to her at all. I just wanted to strangle her again.

This time for good.

I mean, how much can one girl take in a day? Judith had tripped me in math class, dumped her disgusting tapioca pudding all over my new Doc

Martens in Home Ec., and kicked me unconscious in basketball practice.

Did I really have to smile and accept her apology now?

No way! No way in a million years.

I trudged silently to the locker room, my head bent, my eyes on the floor.

When she saw that I wasn't going to buy her cheap apology, Judith got angry. *Do you believe that?* She shoves her knee through my chest — then *she* gets angry!

"Why don't you just fly away, Byrd!" she muttered. Then she went trotting back to the gym floor.

I got changed without showering. Then I collected my stuff, slunk out of the building, and got my bike.

That's really the last straw, I thought, walking my bike across the parking lot in back of school.

It was about half an hour later. The late afternoon sky was gray and overcast. I felt a few light drops of rain on my head.

The last straw, I repeated to myself.

I live two blocks from the school, but I didn't feel like going home. I felt like riding and riding and riding. I felt like just going straight and never turning back.

I was angry and upset and shaky. But mainly angry.

19

Ignoring the raindrops, I climbed onto my bike and began pedaling in the direction away from my house. Front yards and houses went by in a whir. I didn't see them. I didn't see anything.

I pedaled harder and harder. It felt so good to get away from school. To get away from Judith.

The rain started to come down a little harder. I didn't mind. I raised my face to the sky as I pedaled. The raindrops felt cold and refreshing on my hot skin.

When I looked down, I saw that I had reached Jeffers' Woods, a long stretch of trees that divides my neighborhood from the next.

A narrow bike path twisted through the tall, old trees, which were winter bare and looked sort of sad and lonely without their leaves. Sometimes I took the path, seeing how fast I could ride over its curves and bumps.

But the sky was darkening, the black clouds hovering lower. And I saw a glimmering streak of lightning in the sky over the trees.

I decided I'd better turn around and ride home.

But as I turned, someone stepped in front of me.

A woman!

I gasped, startled to see someone on this empty road by the woods.

I squinted at her as the rain began to fall harder, pattering on the pavement around me. She wasn't young, and she wasn't old. She had dark eyes, like two black pieces of coal, on a pale face. Her thick black hair flowed loosely behind her.

Her clothing was sort of old-fashioned. She had a bright red heavy woolen shawl pulled around her shoulders. She wore a long black skirt down to her ankles.

Her dark eyes seemed to light up as she met my stare.

She looked confused.

I should have run.

I should have pedaled away from her as fast as I could.

If only I had known . . .

But I didn't flee. I didn't escape.

Instead, I smiled at her. "Can I help you?" I asked.

The woman's eyes narrowed. I could see she was checking me out.

I lowered my feet to the ground, balancing the bike between my legs. The rain pattered on the pavement, big cold drops.

I suddenly remembered I had a hood on my windbreaker. So I reached up behind my head and slipped it over my hair.

The sky darkened to an eerie olive color. The bare trees in the woods shivered in a swirling breeze.

The woman took a few steps closer. She was so pale, I thought. Almost ghostlike, except for the deep, dark eyes that were staring so hard at me.

"I — I seem to have lost my way," she said. To my surprise, she had an old woman's voice, sort of shaky and frail.

I squinted at her from under my hood. The rain was matting her thick black hair to her head. It was impossible to tell how old she was. She could have been twenty or sixty!

"This is Montrose Avenue," I told her, speaking loudly because of the drumming of the raindrops. "Actually, Montrose ends here. At the woods."

She nodded thoughtfully, pursing her pale lips. "I am trying to get to Madison," she said. "I think I have completely lost my direction."

"You're pretty far from Madison," I said. "It's way over there." I pointed.

She chewed at her lower lip. "I'm usually pretty good at directions," she said fretfully in her shaky voice. She adjusted the heavy red shawl over her slender shoulders.

"Madison is way over on the east side," I said with a shiver. The rain was cold. I was eager to go home and get into some dry clothes.

"Can you take me there?" the woman asked. She grabbed my wrist.

I almost gasped out loud. Her hand was as cold as ice!

"Can you take me there?" she repeated, bringing her face close to mine. "I would be ever so grateful."

She had taken her hand away. But I could still feel the icy grip on my wrist.

Why didn't I run away?

Why didn't I raise my feet to the pedals and ride out of there as fast as I could?

"Sure. I'll show you where it is," I said.

"Thank you, dear." She smiled. She had a dimple in one cheek when she smiled. I realized she was kind of pretty, in an old-fashioned way.

I climbed off my bike and, holding onto the handlebars, began to walk it. The woman stepped beside me, adjusting her shawl. She walked in the middle of the street, her eyes trained on me.

The rain continued to come down. I saw another jagged bolt of lightning far away in the olive sky. The swirling wind made my windbreaker flap against my legs.

"Am I going too fast?" I asked.

"No, dear. I can keep up," she replied with a smile. She had a small purple bag slung over her shoulder. She protected the bag by tucking it under her arm.

She wore black boots under the long skirt. The boots, I saw, had tiny buttons running up the sides. The boots clicked on the wet pavement as we walked.

"I am sorry to be so much trouble," the woman said, again pursing her lips fretfully.

"No trouble," I replied. *My good deed for the day*, I thought, brushing a drop of rain off my nose.

"I love the rain," she said, raising her hands to it, letting the raindrops splash her open

24

palms. "Without the rain, what would wash the evil away?"

That's a weird thing to say, I thought. I muttered a reply. I wondered what evil she was talking about.

Her long black hair was completely soaked, but she didn't seem to mind. She walked quickly with long, steady strides, swinging one hand as she walked, protecting the purple bag under the other arm.

A few blocks later, the handlebars slipped out of my hands. My bike toppled over, and the pedal scraped my knee as I tried to grab the bike before it fell.

What a klutz!

I pulled the bike up and began walking it again. My knee throbbed. I shivered. The wind blew the rain into my face.

What am I doing out here? I asked myself.

The woman kept walking quickly, a thoughtful expression on her face. "It's quite a rain," she said, gazing up at the dark clouds. "This is so nice of you, dear."

"It isn't too far out of my way," I said politely. *Just eight or ten blocks!*

"I don't know how I could have gone so far astray," she said, shaking her head. "I was sure I was headed in the right direction. Then when I came to those woods . . ."

"We're almost there," I said.

"What is your name?" she asked suddenly.

"Samantha," I told her. "But everyone calls me Sam."

"My name is Clarissa," she offered. "I'm the Crystal Woman."

I wasn't sure I'd heard that last part correctly. I puzzled over it, then let it slip from my mind.

It was late, I realized. Mom and Dad might already be home from work. Even if they weren't, my brother, Ron, was probably home, wondering where I was.

A station wagon rolled toward us, its headlights on. I shielded my eyes from the bright lights and nearly dropped my bike again.

The woman was still walking in the center of the street. I moved toward the curb so she could move out of the station wagon's path. But she didn't seem to care about it. She kept walking straight, her expression not changing, even though the bright headlights were in her face.

"Look out!" I cried.

I don't know if she heard me.

The station wagon swerved to avoid her and honked its horn as it rolled by.

She smiled warmly at me as we kept walking. "So good of you to care about a total stranger," she said.

The streetlights flashed on suddenly. They made the wet street glow. The bushes and hedges,

26

the grass, the sidewalks — everything seemed to glow. It all looked unreal.

"Here we are. This is Madison," I said, pointing to the street sign. *Finally!* I thought.

I just wanted to say good-bye to this strange woman and pedal home as fast as I could.

Lightning flickered. Closer this time.

What a dreary day, I thought with a sigh.

Then I remembered Judith.

The whole miserable day suddenly rolled through my mind again. I felt a wave of anger sweep over me.

"Which way is east?" the woman asked, her shaky voice breaking into my bitter thoughts.

"East?" I gazed both ways on Madison, trying to clear Judith from my mind. I pointed.

The wind picked up suddenly, blowing a sheet of rain against me. I tightened my grip on the handlebars.

"You are so kind," the woman said, wrapping the shawl around her. Her dark eyes stared hard into mine. "So kind. Most young people aren't kind like you."

"Thank you," I replied awkwardly. The cold made me shiver again. "Well . . . good-bye." I started to climb onto my bike.

"No. Wait," she pleaded. "I want to repay you."

"Huh?" I uttered. "No. Really. You don't have to."

"I want to repay you," the woman insisted. She grabbed my wrist again. And again I felt a shock of cold.

"You've been so kind," the woman repeated. "So kind to a total stranger."

I tried to free my wrist, but her grip was surprisingly tight. "You don't have to thank me," I said.

"I want to repay you," she replied, bringing her face close to mine, still holding onto my wrist. "Tell you what. I'll grant you three wishes."

She's crazy, I realized.

I stared into those coal-black eyes. Rainwater trickled from her hair, down the sides of her pale face. I could feel the coldness of her hand, even through the sleeve of my windbreaker.

The woman is crazy, I thought.

I've been walking through the pouring rain for twenty minutes with a crazy person.

"Three wishes," the woman repeated, lowering her voice as if not wanting to be overheard by anyone.

"No. Thanks. I've really got to get home," I said. I tugged my wrist from her grasp and turned to my bike.

"I'll grant you three wishes," the woman repeated. "Anything you wish shall come true." She moved the purple bag in front of her and carefully pulled something from it. It was a glass ball, bright red, the size of a large grapefruit. It sparkled despite the darkness around us.

"That's nice of you," I said, wiping water off the bike seat with my hand. "But I don't really have any wishes right now."

"Please — let me repay you for your kindness," the woman insisted. She raised the gleaming red ball in one hand. Her hand was small and as pale as her face, the fingers bony. "I really do want to repay you."

"My — uh — mom will be worried," I said, glancing up and down the street.

No one in sight.

No one to protect me from this lunatic if she turned dangerous.

Just how crazy was she? I wondered. *Could she be dangerous? Was I making her angry by not playing along, by not making a wish?*

"It isn't a joke," the woman said, reading the doubt in my eyes. "Your wishes will come true. I promise you." She narrowed her gaze. The red ball suddenly glowed brighter. "Make your first wish, Samantha."

I stared back at her, thinking hard. I was cold and wet and hungry — and a little frightened. I just wanted to get home and get dry.

What if she won't let me go?

What if I can't get rid of her? What if she follows me home?

Again, I searched up and down the block. Most of the houses had lights on. I could probably run to the nearest one and get help if I needed it.

30

But, I decided, it might be easier just to play along with the crazy woman and make a wish.

Maybe that would satisfy her, and she'd go on her way and let me go home.

"What is your wish, Samantha?" she demanded. Her black eyes glowed red, the same color as the gleaming ball in her hand.

She suddenly looked very old. Ancient. Her skin was so pale and tight, I thought I could see her skull underneath.

I froze.

I couldn't think of a wish.

And then I blurted out, "My wish is . . . to be the strongest player on my basketball team!"

I don't know why I said that. I guess I was just nervous. And I had Judith on my mind and all that had happened that day, ending up with the *disaster* at basketball practice.

And so that was my wish. Of course I immediately felt like a total jerk. I mean, of all the things to wish for in the world, why would anyone pick that?

But the woman didn't seem at all surprised.

She nodded, closing her eyes for a moment. The red ball glowed brighter, brighter, until the fiery red radiated around me. Then it quickly faded.

Clarissa thanked me again, turned, tucked the glass ball back in the purple bag, and began walking quickly away.

I breathed a sigh of relief. I was so glad she was gone!

I jumped on my bike, turned it around, and began pedaling furiously toward home.

A perfect end to a perfect day, I thought bitterly.

Trapped in the rain with a crazy woman.

And the wish?

I knew it was totally stupid.

I knew I'd never have to think about it again.

7

I found myself thinking about the wish at dinner.

I couldn't get over the way the crystal ball had glowed that strange red color.

Mom was trying to get me to take another helping of mashed potatoes, and I was refusing. They were the kind from a box — you know, potato flakes or something — and didn't taste at all like real mashed potatoes.

"Sam, you've got to eat more if you want to grow big and strong," Mom said, holding the potato serving bowl under my nose.

"Mom, I don't *want* to grow any more!" I exclaimed. "I'm already taller than you are, and I'm only twelve!"

"Please don't shout," Dad said, reaching for the string beans. Canned string beans. Mom gets home from work late and doesn't have time to make any *real* food.

"I was tall when I was twelve," Mom said thoughtfully. She passed the potatoes to Dad.

"And then you shrunk!" Ron exclaimed, snickering. My older brother thinks he's a riot.

"I just meant I was tall for my age," Mom said.

"Well, I'm *too* tall for my age," I grumbled. "I'm too tall for *any* age!"

"In a few years you won't be saying that," Mom told me.

When she looked away, I reached under the table and fed some string beans to Punkin. Punkin is my dog, a little brown mutt. He'll eat *anything*.

"Are there more meatballs?" Dad asked. He knew there were. He just wanted Mom to get up and get them for him.

Which she did.

"How was basketball practice?" Dad asked me.

I made a face and gave a double thumbs-down.

"She's too tall for basketball," Ron mumbled with a mouth full of food.

"Basketball takes stamina," Dad said. Sometimes I can't figure out why Dad says half the things he says.

I mean, what am *I* supposed to say to that?

I suddenly thought of the crazy woman and the wish I had made. "Hey, Ron, want to shoot a few baskets after dinner?" I asked, poking my string beans around on the plate with my fork.

We have a hoop on the front of the garage and floodlights to light up the driveway. Ron and I play a little one-on-one sometimes after dinner. You know. To unwind before starting our homework.

Ron glanced out of the dining room window. "Did it stop raining?"

"Yeah. It stopped," I told him. "About half an hour ago."

"It'll still be real wet," he said.

"A few puddles won't ruin your game," I told him, laughing.

Ron's a really good basketball player. He's a natural athlete. So of course he has almost no interest at all in playing with me. He'd rather stay up in his room reading a book. Any book.

"I've got a lot of homework," Ron said, pushing his black-framed glasses up on his nose.

"Just a few minutes," I pleaded. "Just a little shooting practice."

"Help your sister," Dad urged. "You can give her some pointers."

Ron reluctantly agreed. "But only for a few minutes." He glanced out the window again. "We're going to get soaked."

"I'll bring a towel," I said, grinning.

"Don't let Punkin out," Mom said. "He'll get his paws all wet and track mud on the floor."

"I can't believe we're doing this," Ron grumbled.

I knew it was stupid, but I had to see if my wish had come true.

Would I suddenly be a great basketball player? Would I suddenly be able to outshoot Ron? To actually throw the basketball into the basket?

Would I be able to dribble without stumbling? To pass the ball in the direction I wanted? To catch the ball without it bouncing off my chest?

I kept scolding myself for even thinking about the wish.

It was so dumb. So totally dumb.

Just because a crazy woman offers to grant three wishes, I told myself, *doesn't mean that you have to get all excited and think you're instantly going to turn into Michael Jordan!*

Still, I couldn't wait to play with Ron.

Was I in for a big surprise?

Yes. I *was* in for a surprise.

My shooting was actually *worse*!

The first two times I tossed the ball at the hoop, I missed the garage entirely and had to go chase the ball over the wet grass.

Ron laughed. "I see you've been practicing!" he teased.

I gave him a hard shove in the stomach with the wet basketball. He deserved it. It wasn't funny.

I was so disappointed.

I told myself over and over that wishes don't come true, especially wishes granted by crazy women out wandering in the rain.

Still, I couldn't help but get my hopes up.

I mean, Judith and Anna and the other girls on the team were so mean to me. It would be totally terrific to come to the game against Jefferson Elementary tomorrow and suddenly be the star of the team.

The star. Ha-ha.

Ron dribbled the ball to the hoop and made an easy layup. He caught his own rebound and passed the ball to me.

It sailed through my hands and bounced down the driveway. I started running after it, slipped on the wet surface, and fell facedown into a puddle.

Some star.

I'm playing worse*!* I told myself. *Much worse!*

He helped me up. I brushed myself off.

"Remember, this was *your* idea!" he said.

With a determined cry, I grabbed the ball, darted past him, and dribbled furiously to the basket.

I had to make this basket. I *had* to!

But as I went up for my shot, Ron caught up with me. He leaped high, raised his arms, and batted the ball away.

"*Aaaagggh!*"

I let out a frustrated shout. "*I wish you were only a foot tall!*" I cried.

He laughed and ran after the ball.

But I felt a tremor of fear roll down my body.

What have I just done? I asked myself, staring into the darkness of the backyard, waiting for Ron to return with the ball. *Have I just made my second wish?*

I didn't mean to! I told myself, my heart

thudding wildly in my chest. *It was an accident. It wasn't a real wish.*

Have I just shrunk my brother down to a foot tall?

No. No. No. I repeated over and over, waiting for him to reappear.

The *first* wish hadn't come true. There was no reason to expect the second wish would come true.

I squinted into the heavy darkness of the backyard. "Ron — where are you?"

Then I gasped as he came scampering toward me over the grass — a foot tall — just as I had wished!

I froze like a statue. I felt cold as stone.

Then, as the tiny figure emerged from the darkness, I started to laugh.

"Punkin!" I cried. "How did *you* get out?"

I was so happy to see him — so happy it wasn't a tiny Ron scampering over the grass — I picked up the little dog and hugged him tight.

Of course his paws got me covered with wet mud. But I didn't care.

Sam, you've just got to chill, I scolded myself as Punkin struggled free. *Your wish about Ron couldn't come true because Clarissa isn't here with her glowing red ball.*

You've got to stop thinking about the three wishes, I told myself. *It's just dumb. And you're making yourself crazy over them.*

"What's going on? How'd *he* get out?" Ron cried, appearing from the side of the garage with the ball.

"Must've sneaked out," I replied with a shrug.

We played a few more minutes. But it was cold and wet. And no fun at all, especially for me.

I didn't sink a single basket.

We finished with a foul-shot competition, a short game of HORSE. Ron won easily. I was still on the O.

As we trotted back to the house, Ron patted me on the back. "Ever think of taking up tiddlywinks?" he teased. "Or maybe Parcheesi?"

I uttered an unhappy wail. I had the sudden urge to tell him why I felt so disappointed, to tell him about the weird woman and the three wishes.

I hadn't told Mom or Dad about her, either. The whole story was just too stupid.

But I thought maybe my brother would find it funny. "I have to tell you about this afternoon," I said as we pulled off our wet sneakers in the kitchen. "You won't believe what happened to me. I — "

"Later," he said, pulling off his wet socks and tucking them into the sneakers. "I've got to get to that homework."

He disappeared up to his room.

I started to my room, but the phone rang. I picked it up after the first ring.

It was Cory, calling to ask how my basketball practice had gone after school.

"Great," I told him sarcastically. "Just great. I was so fabulous, they're going to retire my number."

"You don't have a number," Cory reminded me. What a friend.

Judith tried to trip me in the lunchroom the next afternoon. But this time I managed to step over her outstretched sneaker.

I made my way past Judith's table and found Cory nearly hidden in the corner near the trash baskets. He had already unwrapped his lunch and had a very unhappy expression on his face.

"Not grilled cheese again!" I exclaimed, dropping my brown paper lunch bag on the table and pulling out the chair across from him.

"Grilled cheese again," he muttered. "And look at it. I don't even think it's American cheese. I think my dad tried to slip in cheddar on me."

I opened my chocolate-milk carton, then pulled my chair in closer. Across the room, some boys were laughing loudly, tossing a pink-haired Troll doll back and forth. It landed in someone's soup, and the table erupted in wild cheers.

As I picked up my sandwich, a shadow fell over the table. I realized that someone was standing behind me.

"Judith!" I cried, turning my head.

She sneered down at me. She was wearing a green-and-white school sweater over dark green corduroys. "Are you coming to the game after school, Byrd?" she demanded coldly.

I set down the sandwich. "Yeah. Of course I'm coming," I replied, puzzled by the question.

"Too bad," she replied, frowning. "That means we don't have a chance of winning."

Judith's pal Anna suddenly appeared beside her. "Couldn't you get sick or something?" she asked me.

"Hey, give Sam a break!" Cory cried angrily.

"We really want to beat Jefferson," Anna said, ignoring him. She had dark red lipstick smeared on her chin. Anna wore more lipstick than all the other seventh-graders put together.

"I'll try my best," I replied through clenched teeth.

They both laughed as if I had made a joke. Then they walked off, shaking their heads.

If only my stupid wish would come true! I thought bitterly.

But of course I knew that it wouldn't.

I figured I was in for more embarrassment and humiliation at the game.

I had no idea just how surprising the game would turn out to be.

10

The game felt weird from the beginning.

The Jefferson team was mostly sixth-graders, and they were pretty small. But they were well coached. They really seemed to know where they were going. And they had a lot of energy and team spirit.

As they came trotting to the center of the gym for the opening tip-off, my stomach was fluttery and I felt as if I weighed a thousand pounds.

I was really dreading this game. I knew I was going to mess up. And I knew that Judith and Anna would be sure to let me know just how badly I messed up, and how I let the team down.

So I was really shaky as the game started. And when, in the opening tip-off, the ball was slapped right to me, I grabbed it — and started dribbling toward the wrong basket!

Luckily, Anna grabbed me and turned me around before I could shoot a basket for Jefferson!

But I could hear players on both teams laughing. And I glanced at the sidelines and saw that both coaches — Ellen and the Jefferson coach — were laughing, too.

I could feel my face turn beet-red. I wanted to quit right then and go sink into a hole in the ground and never come out.

But — to my amazement — I still had the ball.

I tried to pass it to Judith. But I threw it too low, and a Jefferson girl stole it and started dribbling to our basket.

The game was ten seconds old, and I'd already made two mistakes!

I kept telling myself it was just a game, but it didn't really help. Every time I heard someone laugh I knew they were laughing at me, at how I'd started the game by running in the wrong direction.

When I looked up at the score for the first time, it was six to nothing, Jefferson.

The ball suddenly came sailing to me, seemingly from out of nowhere. I grabbed for it, but it slipped out of my hands. One of my teammates took it, dribbled, then passed it back to me.

I took my first shot. It hit the backboard — a triumph for me! — but didn't come near the basket. Jefferson took the rebound. A few seconds later it was eight to nothing.

I'm playing worse than ever! I moaned to myself. I could see Judith glaring angrily at me from across the floor.

I backed up, staying in the corner, away from the basket. I decided to try to keep out of the action as much as possible. Maybe that way I wouldn't embarrass myself quite so much.

After about five minutes into the first quarter, things started to get weird.

The score was twelve to two, Jefferson.

Judith threw the ball inbounds. She meant to throw it to Anna. But Judith's toss was weak, and the ball bounced to a short, blond-haired Jefferson player.

I saw Judith yawn as she ran after the girl.

A few seconds later, the ball was loose, bouncing near the center of the court. Anna made a weak grab for it. But she seemed to be moving in slow motion, and the blond Jefferson player snatched it from her hands.

Anna stood watching her, breathing hard, perspiration running down her forehead. I had to stop and stare. Anna looked *exhausted* — and we'd only been playing five minutes!

The Jefferson team dribbled all the way across the floor, passing the ball from girl to girl, as our players stood and watched.

"Let's go, Mustangs!" Judith cried, trying to rouse everyone. But I saw her yawn again as she walked to the sidelines to throw in the ball.

"Come on, girls! Hustle! Hustle!" Ellen was shouting from the sidelines, her hands cupped around her mouth. "Run, Judith — don't walk! Let's look *alive!*"

Judith sent another feeble throw onto the floor. It bounced away from a Jefferson player. I scooped it up and started to dribble it, running full speed.

Just outside the key, I stopped, turned, and looked for someone to pass it to.

But to my surprise, my teammates were still far behind me, walking slowly, exhaustedly, in my direction.

As the Jefferson players swarmed around me, trying to take the ball away, I took a shot. It hit the rim of the basket — and bounced right back into my hands.

So I took another shot. And missed again.

Judith raised her hands slowly to catch the rebound. But the ball bounced right through her hands. She frowned in surprise but didn't make a move to go after it.

I grabbed the ball, dribbled twice, nearly tripped over it — and shot.

To my amazement, the ball bounced on top of the hoop, landed on the rim, and then dropped through.

"Way to go, Sam!" I heard Ellen shout from the sidelines.

My teammates uttered weak cheers. I watched

47

them go after the Jefferson players, yawning and moving in slow motion, as if in some kind of trance.

"Pick it up! Pick it up!" Ellen was shouting encouragement.

But her words didn't seem to help.

Judith tripped and fell to her knees. As I stared in bewilderment, she didn't get up.

Anna was yawning loudly, walking toward the ball, not running.

My two other Mustang teammates also seemed to be wandering hazily in slow motion, making lame attempts to defend our basket.

Jefferson scored easily.

Judith was still on her knees, her eyes half shut.

What on earth is happening? I wondered.

A long, shrill whistle broke into my thoughts. It took me a while to realize that Ellen had called time out.

"Mustangs — hustle up! Hustle up!" she shouted, motioning for us to cluster around her.

I quickly trotted over to Ellen. Turning back, I saw Judith, Anna, and the others trudging over slowly, yawning, pulling their bodies with great effort.

And as Ellen shouted for everyone to "hustle up," I watched them wearily approach. Then I realized to my amazement *that my wish had come true!*

11

"What is the matter, girls?" Ellen demanded as we huddled on the sidelines. She glanced from player to player, examining each one with concern.

Anna dropped down wearily to the floor, her shoulders slumped. It looked like she could barely keep her eyes open.

Judith leaned her back against the gym's tile wall. She was breathing hard, and beads of sweat rolled down her pale forehead.

"Let's get up some energy," Ellen urged, clapping her hands. "I thought you girls were *pumped* for this game!"

"There's no air in here," one of the players complained.

"I feel so tired," another one said, yawning.

"Maybe we're coming down with something," Anna suggested from down on the floor.

"Do you feel sick, too?" Ellen asked me.

"No," I told her. "I feel okay."

49

Behind me, Judith groaned wearily and tried to push herself away from the wall.

The referee, a high school kid wearing a black-and-white-striped shirt about five sizes too big for him, blew his whistle. He signaled for us to get back out on the floor.

"I don't understand it," Ellen sighed, shaking her head. She helped pull Anna to her feet. "I don't understand it. I really don't."

I understood it.

I understood it perfectly.

My wish had come true. I couldn't believe it! That strange woman really did have some kind of magical powers. And she had granted my wish.

Only not quite the way I had imagined.

I remembered my words so clearly. I had wished to be the strongest player on the basketball team. That meant I wanted the woman to make me a stronger, better player.

Instead, she had made everyone else *weaker*!

I was the same klutzy player I'd always been. I still couldn't dribble, pass, or shoot.

But I was the strongest player on the team!

How could I have been such a jerk? I scolded myself angrily as I trotted back to the center of the gym floor. Wishes *never* turn out the way you want them to.

When I reached center court, I turned back and saw Judith, Anna, and the others trudging onto the floor. Their shoulders were slumped, and they dragged their sneakers over the floor as they walked.

I have to admit I enjoyed it just a little.

I mean, I felt perfectly fine. And they looked so weak and pitiful.

Judith and Anna really deserve it, I told myself. I tried not to grin as they slumped into their places. But maybe I was smiling just a little.

The referee blew his whistle and called for a jump ball to start things off. Judith and a Jefferson player faced each other at the center circle.

The referee tossed the ball up. The Jefferson girl jumped high. Judith made a real effort. I could see the strain on her face.

But her feet didn't even leave the floor.

The Jefferson player batted the ball to one of her teammates, and they headed down the floor with it.

I chased after them, running at full speed. But the rest of my team could only walk.

Jefferson scored with an easy layup.

"Come on, Judith — we can catch them!" I shouted, clapping my hands cheerfully.

Judith glared dully at me. Her green eyes looked faded, kind of washed out.

"Pick it up! Pick it up! Let's go, Mustangs!" I cheered energetically.

I was really enjoying rubbing it in.

Judith could barely bounce the ball inbounds. I picked it up and dribbled all the way down the floor. Under the basket, one of the Jefferson players bumped me from behind as I tried to shoot.

Two foul shots for me.

It took my slow-motion teammates forever to make their way down the floor to line up.

Of course, I missed both of my foul shots.

But I didn't care.

"Let's go, Mustangs!" I shouted, clapping my hands energetically. "Defense! Defense!"

Suddenly, I had become both a player *and* a cheerleader. I was really enjoying being the best player on the team.

Watching Judith and Anna droop around and drag their bodies back and forth like tired losers was the biggest hoot! It was just awesome!

We lost the game by twenty-four points.

Judith, Anna, and the others looked glad it was over. I started to trot to the locker room to get changed, a big smile on my face.

I was nearly changed by the time my teammates dragged into the locker room. Judith walked up to me and leaned against my locker. She eyed me suspiciously.

"How come *you're* so peppy?" she demanded.

I shrugged. "I don't know," I told her. "I feel okay. Same as ever."

Sweat was pouring down Judith's forehead. Her red hair was matted wetly against her head.

"What's going on here, Byrd?" she demanded, yawning. "I don't get it."

"Maybe you're coming down with the flu or something," I said, trying to hide how much I was enjoying this.

This was *great!*

"Ohhh, I'm so tired," Anna moaned, coming up behind Judith.

"I'm sure you'll both feel better tomorrow," I chirped.

"There's something weird going on here," Judith murmured weakly. She tried to stare hard at me, but her eyes were too tired to focus.

"See you tomorrow!" I said brightly, picking up my stuff and heading out. "Feel better, guys!"

I stopped outside the locker room door.

They will *feel better tomorrow*, I assured myself. *They'll be back to normal tomorrow.*

They won't stay like this — right?

Right??

The next day, the bad news hit me like a ton of bricks.

Judith and Anna weren't in school the next morning.

I stared at their empty seats as I made my way to my seat in the front row. I kept turning back, searching for them. But the bell rang, and they weren't there.

Absent. Both absent.

I wondered if the other girls on the team were absent, too.

I felt a cold shiver run down my back.

Were they still weak and tired? Too weak and tired to come to school?

I had a frightening thought: *What if they* never *returned to normal? What if the magic* never *wore off?*

Then I had an even more frightening thought: *What if Judith and Anna and the others got weaker and weaker? What if they kept getting weaker until they* died — *and it was all my fault?*

All my fault. All my fault.

I felt cold all over. My stomach felt as if I'd swallowed a rock. I had never felt so guilty, so horribly guilty, in all my life.

I tried to force these thoughts from my mind, but I couldn't.

I couldn't stop thinking that they might *die* because of my careless wish.

I'll be a murderer, I told myself with a shudder. *A* murderer.

Sharon, our teacher, was standing right in front of me, talking about something. I couldn't hear a word she said. I kept turning in my seat, staring back at the two empty chairs.

Judith and Anna — what have I done to you?

At lunch, I told the whole story to Cory.

Of course he just laughed at me. He had a mouthful of grilled cheese and nearly choked.

"Do you believe in the Easter Bunny, too?" he asked.

But I was in no mood for jokes. I was really upset. I stared down at my uneaten lunch and felt sick.

"Please take me seriously, Cory," I begged. "I know it sounds dumb — "

"You mean you're for *real*?" he asked, his eyes studying my face. "I thought you were kidding, Sam. I thought this was a story for creative writing or something."

I shook my head. "Listen, Cory — if you had been at the girls' basketball game yesterday afternoon, you'd know I'm not kidding," I said, leaning across the table and whispering. "They were dragging around as if they were sleepwalking," I told him. "It was so eerie!"

I was so upset, my shoulders started to shake. I covered my eyes to keep myself from crying.

"Okay . . . let's think about this," Cory said softly, his funny, crooked smile fading to a thoughtful frown. Finally, he had decided to take me seriously.

"I've been thinking and thinking about it all morning," I told him, still trying to force back the tears. "What if I'm a *murderer*, Cory? What if they really *die*?"

"Sam, please," he said, still frowning, his dark brown eyes studying mine. "Judith and Anna are probably not even sick. You're probably making this all up in your mind. They're probably perfectly okay."

"No way," I muttered glumly.

"Oh. I know!" Cory's face brightened. "We can ask Audrey."

"Audrey?" Audrey was the school nurse. It took me a while to figure out what Cory was thinking. But I finally did.

He was right. When you were going to be absent, your parents had to call Audrey in the morning and tell her why. Most likely, Audrey would be able to tell us why Judith and Anna were not in school today.

I jumped up, nearly knocking my chair over. "Great idea, Cory!" I exclaimed. I started running through the lunchroom toward the door.

"Wait! I'll come with you!" Cory called, hurrying to catch up.

Our sneakers pounded against the hard floor as we made our way down the long hall to the nurse's office. We found Audrey locking the door.

She is a short, sort of chunky woman, about forty or so, I guess, with bleached-blond hair pinned up in a bun on top of her head. She always wears baggy jeans and shaggy sweaters, never a nurse's uniform.

"Lunchtime," she said, seeing us stop beside her. "What do they have today? I'm starving."

"Audrey, can you tell us why Judith and Anna aren't in school today?" I demanded breathlessly, ignoring her question.

"Huh?" I was talking so fast, so excitedly, I don't think she understood me.

"Judith Bellwood and Anna Frost?" I repeated, my heart pounding. "Why aren't they in school today?"

I saw surprise in Audrey's pale gray eyes. Then she lowered her gaze.

"Judith and Anna, they're gone," she said sadly.

I stared at her. My mouth dropped open in horror. "They're gone?"

"They're gone for at least a week," Audrey said. She bent to lock the office door.

"They — *what*?" I squeaked.

She had trouble pulling the key from the lock. "They went to the doctor," she repeated. "Their moms called this morning. They're very sick. Both girls have the flu or something. They felt weak. Too weak to come to school."

I breathed a sigh of relief. I was glad Audrey had been concentrating on the door lock, so she hadn't seen the horrified look on my face.

Audrey hurried off down the hall. As soon as she was out of sight, I slumped against the wall. "At least they're not *dead*," I moaned. "She scared me to death!"

Cory shook his head. "Audrey scared me, too," he confessed. "See? Judith and Anna just have the flu. I'm sure the doctors — "

"They don't have the flu," I insisted. "They're weak because of my wish."

"Call them later," he suggested. "You'll see. They'll probably be much better."

"I can't wait till later," I said in a trembling voice. "I have to do something, Cory. I have to do something to keep them from getting weaker and weaker until they shrivel up and die!"

"Calm down, Sam — "

I started pacing back and forth in front of him. Some kids came hurrying by on their way to their lockers. Someone called to me, but I didn't reply.

"We've got to get to class," Cory said. "I think you're getting all weird over nothing, Sam. If you wait till tomorrow — "

"She said I had three wishes!" I exclaimed, not hearing a word Cory was saying. "I only used one."

"Sam — " Cory shook his head disapprovingly.

"I've got to find her!" I decided. "I've got to find that strange woman. Don't you see? I can wish to have the first wish undone. She *said* I get three wishes. So my second wish can be to erase the first!"

This idea was starting to make me feel a lot better.

But then Cory brought me back down into my gloom with one question:

"How are you going to find her, Sam?"

I thought about Cory's question all afternoon. I barely heard a word anyone said to me.

We had a vocab test near the end of the day. I stared at the words as if they were in Martian!

After a while, I heard Lisa, my English teacher, calling my name. She was standing right in front of me, but I don't think I heard her until her fifth or sixth try.

"Are you okay, Samantha?" she asked, leaning over me. I knew she was wondering why I hadn't started my test.

"I feel a little sick," I replied quietly. "I'll be okay.

I'll be okay as soon as I find that weird woman and get her to erase her spell!

But where will I find her? I wondered. *Where?*

After school, I reported to the gym for basketball

practice. Everyone on my team was absent, so practice was canceled.

Absent because of me . . .

I trudged upstairs to my locker and retrieved my down jacket. As I slammed the door and locked it, I had an idea.

The woods. Jeffers' Woods.

That's where I'd found Clarissa.

I'll bet I can find her there again.

Maybe it's her secret meeting place, I thought. *Maybe she'll be waiting for me there.*

Of course, *she will!* I told myself, giving myself a pep talk. Why did it take me so long to think of this? It made perfect sense.

Humming to myself, I started jogging to the door. The hallway was nearly empty.

I stopped when I saw a familiar figure in the doorway. "Mom!"

"Hi, Sam." She waved to me, even though I was standing right in front of her. She had a red-and-white wool cap pulled over her short blond hair, and she was wearing the tattered red ski jacket she always wears.

She hadn't been skiing in years. But she liked dressing like a ski bum.

"Mom — what are you doing here?" I cried, not meaning it to sound as unfriendly as it did. I was eager to get to my bike and ride to Jeffers' Woods. I didn't need *her* here!

"You didn't forget about your appointment with Dr. Stone?" she asked, waving her car keys in her hand.

"The orthodontist? Today?" I cried. "I *can't*!"

"You have to," she replied sternly, tugging the arm of my jacket. "You know how hard it is to get in to see Dr. Stone."

"But I don't *want* braces!" I cried, realizing I was sounding a little shrill, a little babyish.

"Maybe you won't need them," Mom said, pulling me to the door. "Maybe you can get by with just a retainer. We'll do whatever Dr. Stone says."

"But Mom — I — I — " I searched my mind for an excuse. "I can't go with you. I have my bike here!" I cried desperately.

"Go get it. We'll put it in the trunk," she replied without blinking.

I had no choice. I had to go with her. Sighing loudly, I pushed open the door and hurried past her toward the bike racks.

I found out I'm going to be wearing braces for at least the next six months. I had another appointment with Dr. Stone the next week to have them put on.

I suppose I should have been upset about it. But it was hard to think about braces with Judith, Anna, and the other girls on my mind.

I kept picturing them wasting away, getting thinner and thinner, weaker and weaker. I kept seeing this terrifying image in my mind. I was in the gym, dribbling the ball back and forth, faster and faster. And Judith, Anna, and the others were lying flat on their backs on the bleachers, trying to watch but too weak to hold their heads up.

That night after dinner, I was feeling so guilty, I called Judith to see how she was feeling. I think it was the first time in my life I had ever called her.

Mrs. Bellwood answered. She sounded tired and tense. "Who is this?" she asked.

I had a sudden impulse to hang up. But I told her, "It's Samantha Byrd. I'm a friend from school."

Some friend.

"I don't think Judith can come to the phone," she replied. "She's just so weak."

"Did the doctor say what — ?" I started.

"I'll ask Judith if she wants to talk," Mrs. Bellywood interrupted. I could hear Judith's little brother shouting something in the background. And I could hear cartoon music from their TV. "Don't stay on too long," she instructed.

"Hello?" Judith answered in a faint, little-girl voice.

"Oh. Hi, Judith. It's me. Sam," I said, trying not to sound nervous.

"Sam?" Again the faint voice, nearly a whisper.

"Sam Byrd," I stammered. "I — I just wondered how you were feeling."

"Sam, did you cast a spell on us?" Judith asked.

I gasped. *How did she know?*

"Judith — what do you mean?" I sputtered.

"All the girls are sick except for you," Judith replied. "Anna is sick. And so is Arlene. And Krista."

"Yes, but that doesn't mean — " I started.

"So I think you cast a spell on us," Judith interrupted.

Was she joking? I couldn't tell.

"I just hope you feel better," I mumbled awkwardly. I could hear Mrs. Bellwood in the background telling Judith she should get off the phone.

So I said good-bye and hung up. I was grateful it was a short conversation. But I couldn't decide if Judith was kidding or not about my casting a spell.

Her voice was really weak. She sounded so weary and lifeless.

I felt angry that she had accused me, joke or no joke. That was so typical of Judith. Finding a way to make me angry even when I was calling to be nice.

But I also felt guilty. Whether Judith had guessed it or not, I *had* cast a spell on her and the others.

And now I had to find a way to have the spell removed.

The next morning, two seats in my class were empty again. Judith and Anna were both absent.

At lunch, I asked Cory if he wanted to come with me after school to go searching for the strange woman.

"No way!" he cried, shaking his head. "She'll probably turn me into a frog or something!"

"Cory — can't you take this seriously?" I screamed. Several kids turned to look.

"Give me a break," Cory muttered, blushing under his Orlando Magic cap.

"Okay, I'm sorry," I told him. "I'm really stressed out — you know?"

He still refused to keep me company. He made up a lame excuse about having to help his mother clean the basement.

Who cleans the basement in the middle of winter?

Cory pretended he didn't believe my story about the woman and the three wishes. But I had the feeling that maybe he was a little afraid.

I was afraid, too. Afraid I wouldn't find her.

After school, I jumped on my bike and began pedaling toward Jeffers' Woods.

It was a gray, blustery day. Enormous dark clouds rolled rapidly over the sky, threatening rain, maybe snow.

It's a lot like the day I ran into Clarissa, I thought. For some reason, that fact encouraged me.

Some kids in my class waved to me and called out. But I rode past them, leaning over the handlebars, shifting gears to pick up speed.

A few minutes later, Montrose Avenue curved away from the houses that lined both sides, and the bare trees of the woods came into view.

The tall trees formed a dark wall, darker than the charcoal sky above.

"She's got to be here, got to be here," I repeated in rhythm with my pedaling feet.

Got to be here, got to be here.

My heart nearly leaped out of my chest when I saw her, huddled low at the edge of the road. Waiting for me.

"Hi!" I called out. "Hi! It's me!"

Why didn't she answer?

As I pedaled closer, my heart pounding happily, I saw that she had her back turned to me.

She had changed her outfit. She was wearing a purple wool beret and a long black coat down nearly to her ankles.

I screeched my bike to a halt a few feet behind her, my tires skidding over the pebbly road. "I need to make another wish!" I called breathlessly.

She turned, and I gasped.

I stared into a face full of freckles, a young-looking face framed by short, curly blond hair.

"I'm sorry. What did you say?" she asked, narrowing her eyes at me, her expression bewildered.

"I — I'm sorry," I stammered, feeling my face turn hot. "I — I thought you were some-one else."

It was a different woman.

I felt so embarrassed, I just wanted to die!

Behind her, I saw two blond-haired kids tossing a Frisbee back and forth at the edge of the woods. "Tommy — don't throw it so hard. Your sister can't catch it!" the woman instructed.

Then she turned back to me. "What did you say about wishes? Are you lost?" she asked, studying my face with concern.

I knew I was still blushing, but I couldn't help it. "No. I thought you were — " I started.

"Tommy — go chase it yourself!" she shouted to her little boy. The two kids started squabbling. She hurried over to settle it.

"Sorry I bothered you," I called. "Bye." I turned my bike around and started pedaling rapidly toward home.

I was embarrassed that I'd said such a stupid thing to a total stranger. But mainly I was disappointed.

I really had expected the strange woman to be there.

Where else could she be? I asked myself.

I remembered that I had shown her the way to Madison Road. *Maybe*, I decided, *I will get lucky and run into her there.*

It was a real long shot. But I was desperate.

I turned my bike around and made my way to Madison. The wind had picked up, and my face began to feel cold and raw. I was riding against the wind, and the sharp cold was making my eyes water.

Even through the blur, I could see that the woman was not hanging around on Madison, waiting for me to show up.

Two mangy brown mutts trotted side by side across the street, their heads bowed against the wind. They were the only living creatures I saw.

I rode slowly back and forth a few times, my eyes searching the rambling old houses of the neighborhood.

A total waste of time.

I was completely frozen. My ears and nose tingled with numbness. My watering eyes sent cold tears rolling down my cheeks.

"Give up, Sam," I instructed myself aloud.

The sky darkened. The storm clouds hovered low above the shivering trees.

Feeling miserable and defeated, I turned and headed for home. I was pedaling furiously down the center of the street, trying to keep my bike upright in the gusting wind.

I stopped when Judith's house came into view. It was a long, low, redwood ranch-style house set back from the street on a wide, sloping front lawn.

Maybe I'll stop for a minute and see how Judith is doing, I decided.

It'll give me a chance to get warm, too, I thought. I reached up a hand and felt my nose. Totally numb.

Shivering, I rode up the driveway and lowered my bike to the ground. Then, trying to rub some feeling into my poor nose, I jogged up the walk and rang the bell.

Mrs. Bellwood seemed very surprised to see a visitor. I told her who I was and that I just happened to be riding by. "How is Judith feeling?" I asked, shivering.

"About the same," she replied with a worried sigh. She had Judith's green eyes, but her hair was nearly entirely gray.

She led me into the hallway, which felt toasty and warm. The house smelled of roasting chicken. I suddenly realized I was hungry.

"Judith! You have a visitor!" Mrs. Bellwood shouted up the stairs.

I heard a weak reply, but couldn't make out the words.

"Go on up," Judith's mother said, putting a hand on the shoulder of my coat. "You look so cold," she added, shaking her head. "Be careful, dear. You don't want to get sick, too."

I climbed the stairs and found Judith's room at the end of the hall. I hesitated at the doorway and peered in.

The room was dimly lit. I could see Judith lying in bed, on top of the quilt, her head propped up on several pillows. Books and magazines and a couple of school notebooks were scattered over the bed.

But Judith wasn't reading. She was just staring straight ahead.

"Stork?" she cried, seeing me in the doorway.

I entered the room, forcing a smile to my face. "How are you feeling?" I asked softly.

"What are *you* doing here?" she asked coldly. Her voice was hoarse.

"I — I was riding my bike, and — " I stammered, staying by the door. I was startled by her anger.

"Riding your bike? In this cold?" With great effort, she pulled herself up to a sitting position. Leaning against the headboard, she glared at me suspiciously.

"I just wondered how you were," I muttered.

"Why don't you just fly away, Byrd!" she growled nastily.

"Huh?"

"You *are* a witch — aren't you!" she accused.

I couldn't believe she was saying these things. I was stunned. Shocked! It was no joke. I could see clearly that she was serious!

"You *did* cast a spell on us. I know it!"

"Judith — please," I cried. "What are you *saying*?"

"We did a unit on witches in social studies last year," she said in her hoarse voice. "We studied spells and things."

"That's crazy!" I insisted.

"You were jealous of me, Sam. Of me and Anna and everyone else," Judith accused.

"So?" I cried angrily.

"So, all of a sudden all the girls on the team feel weak and sick. Except for you, Sam. You feel fine — right?"

"Judith, listen to me — " I pleaded.

"You're a witch, Sam!" she screamed, her weak voice breaking. She started to cough.

"Judith, you're talking like a crazy person," I insisted. "I'm not a witch. How could I be a witch? I'm sorry you're sick. Really, I am. But — "

"You're a witch! You're a witch!" Judith chanted, her voice a shrill whisper. "I've talked to all the girls. They all agree. You're a witch. A witch!"

I was so furious, I thought I'd explode. I had my hands balled into tight fists. My head was throbbing.

Judith had been talking to all the other girls, spreading this story that I was a witch. How could she do such a crazy thing?

"A witch! You're a witch!" she continued to chant.

I was so upset, I totally lost it. *"Judith —"* I shrieked. *"I — I never would have done it to you if you hadn't been so horrible to me!"*

I realized immediately that I'd made a terrible mistake.

I had just admitted to her that I *was* responsible for her being sick.

I had just blurted out that I *was* a witch!

But I was so furious, I didn't care.

"I *knew* it!" Judith croaked in her hoarse voice, her green eyes glowing excitedly, pointing an accusing finger at me.

"What's going on here? What's all the shouting?" Judith's mother appeared in the room, her eyes flashing back and forth between Judith and me.

"She's a witch! A witch!" Judith screamed.

"Judith — your voice! Stop!" Mrs. Bellwood cried, running to the bed. She turned back to me. "I think Judith is delirious. She — she's saying such crazy things. Please don't pay attention. She — "

"She's a witch! She admitted it! She's a witch!" Judith shrieked.

"Judith — please. Please, you have to calm down. You have to save your strength," Mrs. Bellwood pleaded.

"I'm sorry. I'll go now," I said sharply.

I darted out of the room and ran down the stairs and out of the house as fast as I could.

"*A witch! A witch!*" Judith's hoarse chant followed me out.

I was so angry, so hurt, so humiliated, I felt about to explode. "I wish Judith would *disappear!*" I screamed. "I really do!"

"Very well. That shall be your second wish," said a voice behind me.

I spun around to see the strange woman standing at the side of the house, her long black hair fluttering behind her in the gusting wind. She held the glowing red ball high. Her eyes glowed as red as the ball.

"I shall cancel your first wish," she said in her shaky old lady's voice. "And I shall grant your second."

"No — wait!" I cried.

The woman smiled and pulled her shawl over her head.

"Wait! I didn't mean it!" I cried, running toward her. "I didn't know you were there. Wait — OW!"

My foot caught on a loose stone in the walk, and I stumbled. I hit my knees hard. The pain shot up through my entire body.

When I looked up, she was gone.

After dinner, Ron agreed to play basketball out back. But it was too cold and windy. A light snow had started to fall.

We settled for Ping-Pong in the basement.

Ping-Pong games in our basement are always difficult. For one thing, the ceiling is so low, the ball is always hitting it and bouncing crazily away. Also, Punkin has a bad habit of chasing after the ball and biting holes in it.

Ping-Pong is the only sport I'm good at. I have a really tricky serve, and I'm good at slamming the ball down my opponent's throat. I can usually beat Ron two games out of three.

But tonight he could see my heart wasn't in it.

"What's up?" he asked as we batted the ball softly back and forth. His dark eyes peered into mine from behind his black-framed glasses.

I decided I *had* to tell him about Clarissa, and her red crystal ball, and the three wishes. I was so desperate to tell someone.

"I helped this strange woman a few days ago," I blurted out. "And she granted me three wishes, I made a wish, and now all the girls on my basketball team are going to die!"

Ron dropped his paddle onto the table. His mouth dropped open. "What an amazing coincidence!" he cried.

"Huh?" I gaped at him.

"I met my fairy godmother yesterday!" Ron exclaimed. "She promised to make me the richest person in the world, and she's going to give me a solid-gold Mercedes with a swimming pool in the back!"

He burst out laughing. He just thinks he's such a riot.

"*Aaaaagh!*" I let out an angry, frustrated groan.

Then I tossed my paddle at him and ran upstairs to my room.

*   *   *

I slammed the bedroom door behind me and began to pace back and forth, my arms crossed tightly in front of me.

I kept telling myself that I had to calm down, that it wasn't good to be this stressed out. But of course, telling yourself to calm down doesn't do any good. It only makes you more tense.

I decided I had to do something to occupy my mind, to keep myself from thinking about Judith, and Clarissa, and the new wish I had accidentally made.

My second wish.

"It's not fair!" I cried aloud, still pacing.

After all, I didn't know I was making a second wish. That woman tricked me! She appeared out of nowhere — and tricked me!

I stopped in front of my mirror and fiddled with my hair. I have very fine light blond hair. It's so fine, there isn't much I can do with it. I usually tie it in a ponytail on the right side of my head. It's a style I saw on a model that looked a little like me in *Seventeen*.

Just to keep my hands busy, I tried doing something else with my hair. Studying myself in the mirror, I tried sweeping it straight back. Then I tried parting it in the middle and letting it fall over my ears. It looked really lame.

The activity wasn't helping. It wasn't taking my mind off Judith at all. I pulled it back into the

78

same old ponytail. Then I brushed it for a while, tossed down the brush with a sigh, and returned to pacing.

My big question, of course, was: Had my wish come true?

Had I caused Judith to disappear?

As much as I hated Judith, I certainly didn't want to be responsible for making her disappear forever.

With a loud moan, I tossed myself down on my bed. *What should I do?* I asked myself. I *had* to know if the wish had come true.

I decided to call her house.

I wouldn't talk to her. I'd just call her house and see if she was still around.

I wouldn't even tell them who was calling.

I looked up Judith's number in the school directory. I didn't know it by heart. I had only called it once before.

My hand was shaking as I reached for the phone on my desk. I punched in her phone number.

It took me three tries. I kept making mistakes.

I was really scared. I felt as if my stomach were tied in a knot and my heart had jumped up into my throat.

The phone rang. One ring.

Two rings.

Three rings.

Had she disappeared?

Four rings.

No answer.

"She's gone," I murmured aloud, a chill running down my back.

Before the fifth ring could begin, I heard a clicking sound. Someone had picked up the receiver.

"Hello?"

Judith!

"Hello? Who *is* this?" she demanded.

I slammed the receiver down.

My heart was pounding. My hands were ice-cold.

I breathed a sigh of relief. Judith was there. She was definitely there. She hadn't vanished from the face of the earth.

And I realized her voice had returned to normal.

She didn't sound hoarse or weak. She sounded as nasty as ever.

What did this mean? I jumped to my feet and began to pace back and forth, trying to figure it all out.

Of course, I *couldn't* figure it out.

I only knew that the second wish hadn't been granted.

Feeling a little relieved, I went to bed and quickly fell into a heavy, dreamless sleep.

I opened one eye, then the other. Pale morning sunlight was shining through my bedroom window. With a sleepy groan, I pushed down the covers and started to sit up.

My eye went to the clock above my desk and I gasped.

Nearly ten after eight?

I rubbed my eyes and looked again. Yes. Ten after eight.

"Huh?" I cried, trying to clear the sleep from my voice. Mom wakes me every morning at seven so I can get to school by eight-thirty.

What happened?

There was no way I'd be on time now.

"Hey — Mom!" I shouted. "Mom!" I jumped out of bed. My long legs got tangled up in the covers, and I nearly fell over.

Great way to start the day — with a typical Samantha klutz move!

"Hey, Mom — " I shouted out the bedroom door. "What happened? I'm late!"

Not hearing a reply, I pulled off my night-shirt and quickly searched through the closet for some clean clothes to wear. Today was Friday, laundry day. So I was down to the bottom of the pile.

"Hey, Mom? Ron? Anybody up?"

Dad leaves the house for work every morning at seven. Usually I hear him moving around. This morning I hadn't heard a sound.

I pulled on a pair of faded jeans and a pale green sweater. Then I brushed my hair, staring at my still-sleepy face in the mirror.

"Anybody up?" I shouted. "How come no one woke me today? It's not a holiday — is it?"

I listened carefully as I tugged on my Doc Martens.

No radio on down in the kitchen. *How weird*, I thought. *Mom has that radio tuned to the all-news station every morning. We fight about it every morning. She wants news, and I want music.*

But today I couldn't hear a sound down there. *What's going on?*

"Hey — I'm going to have to skip breakfast!" I shouted down the stairs. "I'm late."

No reply.

I took one last look in the mirror, brushed a strand of hair off my forehead, and hurried out into the hall.

My brother's room is next door to mine. His door was closed.

Uh-oh, Ron, I thought. *Did you sleep late, too?* I pounded on the door. "Ron? Ron, are you awake?"

Silence.

"Ron?" I pushed open the door. His room was dark, except for the pale light from the window. The bed was made.

Had Ron already left? Why had he made his bed? It would be the first time in his life he ever did!

"Hey, Mom!" Confused, I hurried down the stairs. Halfway down, I stumbled and nearly fell. Klutz Move Number Two. Pretty good for so early in the morning.

"What's going on down here? Is it the weekend? Did I sleep through Friday?"

The kitchen was empty. No Mom. No Ron. No breakfast.

Did they have to go somewhere early? I checked the refrigerator for a note.

Nothing.

Puzzled, I glanced at the clock. Nearly eight-thirty. I was already late for school.

Why didn't anyone wake me up? Why were they all gone so early in the morning?

I pinched myself. I really did. I thought maybe I was dreaming.

But no such luck.

"Hey — anyone?" I called. My voice rang through the empty house.

I ran to the front closet to get my coat. I had to get to school. I was sure this mystery would be cleared up later.

I quickly pulled on my coat and ran upstairs for my backpack. My stomach was grumbling and growling. I was used to at least a glass of juice and a bowl of cereal for breakfast.

Oh, well, I thought, *I'll buy an extra-big lunch.*

A few seconds later, I headed out the front door and around the side to the garage to get my bike. I pulled up the garage door — and stopped.

I froze, staring into the garage.

My dad's car. It was still in the garage.

He hadn't left for work.

So where was everyone?

Back in the house I phoned my dad's office. The phone rang and rang, and no one answered.

I checked the kitchen again for a message from Mom or Dad. But I couldn't find a thing.

Glancing at the kitchen clock, I saw that I was already twenty minutes late for school. I needed a late-excuse note, but there was no one to write it for me.

I hurried back outside to get my bike. *Better late than never,* I thought. I wasn't exactly frightened. I was just puzzled.

I'll call Mom or Dad at lunchtime and find out where everyone went this morning, I told myself. As I pedaled to school, I began to feel a little angry. They could've at least told me they were leaving early!

There were no cars on the street and no kids on bikes. I guessed that everyone was already at school or work or wherever people go in the morning. I got to school in record time.

Leaving my bike in the bike rack, I adjusted my backpack on my shoulders and ran into the school. The halls were dark and empty. My footsteps echoed loudly on the hard floor.

I dropped my coat into my locker. When I slammed the locker door, it sounded like an explosion in the empty hallway.

The halls are kind of creepy when they're this empty, I thought. I jogged to my classroom, which was just a few doors down from my locker.

"My mom forgot to wake me, so I overslept."

That was the excuse I'd planned to give Sharon as soon as I entered. I mean, it wasn't just an excuse. It was the truth.

But I never got to tell Sharon my reason for being late.

I pulled open the door to the classroom — and stared in shock.

Empty. The room was empty.

No kids. No Sharon.

The lights hadn't been turned on. And yesterday's work was still on the chalkboard.

Weird, I thought.

But I didn't know then how weird things were going to get.

I froze for a moment, staring into the empty, dark room. Then I decided that everyone must be at an assembly in the auditorium.

I turned quickly and made my way to the

auditorium at the front of the school, jogging down the empty corridor.

The door to the teachers' lounge was open. I peered in and was surprised to find it empty, too. *Maybe all the teachers are at the assembly,* I thought.

A few seconds later, I pulled open the double doors to the auditorium.

And peered into the darkness.

The auditorium was silent and empty.

I pushed the doors shut and began to run down the hall, stopping to look into every room.

It didn't take me long to realize that I was the only person in the building. No kids. No teachers. I even checked the janitors' room downstairs. No janitors.

Is it Sunday? Is it a holiday?

I tried to figure out where everyone had gone, but I couldn't.

Feeling the first stirrings of panic in my chest, I dropped a quarter in the pay phone next to the principal's office and called home.

I let it ring at least ten times. Still no one home.

"Where *is* everyone?" I shouted down the empty corridor. The only reply came from my echoing voice.

"Can *anybody* hear me?" I shouted, cupping my hands around my mouth. Silence.

I suddenly felt very frightened. I had to get out of the creepy school building. I grabbed my coat and started to run. I didn't even bother to close the locker door.

Carrying my coat over my shoulder, I ran outside to the bike rack. My bike was the only bike parked there. I scolded myself for not noticing that when I arrived.

I pulled on my coat, arranged my backpack, and started for home. Again, I saw no cars on the street. No people.

"This is so *weird!*" I cried aloud.

My legs suddenly felt heavy, as if something was weighing them down. I knew it was my panic. My heart was pounding. I kept searching desperately for someone — anyone — on the street.

Halfway home, I turned around and headed my bike to town. The small shopping district was just a few blocks north of school.

I rode in the center of the street. There was no reason not to. No cars or trucks appeared in either direction.

The bank came into view, followed by the grocery store. As I pedaled as hard as I could, I noticed all the other shops that lined both sides of Montrose Avenue.

All dark and empty.

Not a soul in town. Not a person in any store. No one.

I braked the bike in front of Farber's Hardware and jumped off. The bike fell onto its side. I stepped to the sidewalk and listened. The only sound was the banging of a shutter being blown by the wind above the barbershop.

"Hello!" I called at the top of my voice. "Helllloooo!"

I started running frantically from store to store, pressing my face against the windows, peering inside, searching desperately for another human being.

Back and forth. I covered both sides of the street, my fear growing heavier inside me with each step. With each dark store.

"Hellooooo! Helllooooo! Can anybody hear me?"

But I knew it was a waste of my voice.

Standing in the center of the street, staring at the dark stores and empty sidewalks, I knew that I was alone.

Alone in the world.

I suddenly realized my second wish had been granted.

Judith had disappeared. *And everyone else had disappeared with her.*

Everyone.

My mom and dad. My brother, Ron. Everyone.

Would I ever see them again?

I slumped down on the cement stoop in front of the barbershop and hugged myself, trying to stop my body from trembling.

Now what? I wondered miserably. *Now what?*

20

I don't know how long I sat there on the stoop, hugging myself, my head lowered, my mind in a total, spinning panic. I would have sat there forever, listening to the banging shutter, listening to the wind blow through the deserted street — if my stomach hadn't started to growl and grumble.

I stood up, suddenly remembering that I had missed my breakfast.

"Sam, you're all alone in the world. How can you think about eating?" I asked myself aloud.

Somehow it was comforting to hear a human voice, even though it was my own.

"I'm staaaaarving!" I shouted.

I listened for a response. It was really stupid, but I refused to give up hope.

"This is all Judith's fault," I muttered, picking my bike up from the street.

I rode home through the empty streets, my eyes searching the deserted yards and houses. As

I passed the Carters' house on the corner of my block, I expected their little white terrier to come yapping after my bike the way he always did.

But there weren't even any dogs left in my world. Not even my poor little Punkin.

There was just me. Samantha Byrd. The last person on earth.

As soon as I got home, I rushed into the kitchen and made myself a peanut butter sandwich. Gobbling it down, I stared at the open peanut butter jar. It was nearly empty.

"How am I going to feed myself?" I wondered aloud. "What do I do when the food runs out?"

I started to fill a glass with orange juice. But I hesitated and filled it up only halfway.

Do I rob the grocery store? I asked myself. *Do I just* take *the food I need?*

Is it really robbing if there's no one there? If there's no one anywhere?

Does it matter? Does anything *matter?*

"How can I take care of myself? I'm only twelve!" I shouted.

For the first time, I felt the urge to cry. But I jammed another hunk of peanut butter sandwich into my mouth and forced the urge away.

Instead, I turned my thoughts to Judith, and my unhappiness and fear quickly gave way to anger.

If Judith hadn't made fun of me, hadn't tried to embarrass me, if Judith hadn't constantly sneered at me and said, "Byrd, why don't you just fly away!" and all the other horrible things she'd said to me, then I never would have made any wishes about her, and I wouldn't be all alone now.

"I hate you, Judith!" I screamed.

I jammed the last section of sandwich into my mouth — but I didn't chew.

I froze. And listened.

I heard something. Footsteps. Someone walking in the living room.

I swallowed the sandwich section whole and went tearing into the living room. "Mom? Dad?"

Were they back? Were they really back?

No.

I stopped in the living room doorway when I saw Clarissa. She was standing in the center of the room, her black hair reflecting the light from the front window, a pleased smile on her face.

Her bright red shawl was draped loosely over her shoulders. She wore a long black jumper over a white high-collared blouse.

"You!" I cried breathlessly. "How did you get in?"

She shrugged. Her smile grew wider.

"Why did you *do* this to me?" I shrieked, my anger bursting out of me. "*How* could you do this to me?" I demanded, gesturing at the empty room, the empty house.

"I didn't," she replied quietly.

She walked to the window. In the bright afternoon sunlight, her skin appeared pale and wrinkled. She looked so old.

"But — but — " I sputtered, too furious to speak.

"You did it," she said, her smile fading. "You made the wish. I granted it."

"I didn't wish for my family to disappear!" I screamed, striding into the room, my hands balled into tight fists. "I didn't wish for *everyone in the world* to disappear! *You* did that! *You!*"

"You wished for Judith Bellwood to disappear," Clarissa said, adjusting the shawl on her shoulders. "I granted the wish as best as I knew how."

"No. You tricked me," I insisted angrily.

She snickered. "Magic is often unpredictable," she said. "I figured you would not be happy with your last wish. That is why I have returned. You have one more wish. Would you like to make it now?"

"Yes!" I exclaimed. "I want my family back. I want all the people back. I — "

"Be careful," she warned, pulling the red glass ball from the purple bag. "Think carefully before you make your final wish. I am trying to repay your kindness to me. I do not want you to be unhappy with the results of your wish."

I started to reply but stopped.

She was right. I had to be careful.

I had to make the right wish this time. And I had to say it the right way.

"Take your time," she urged softly. "Since this is your final wish, it shall be permanent. Be very careful."

I stared into her eyes as they turned from black to red, reflecting the red glow of the ball in her hand, and I thought as hard as I could.

What should I wish for?

22

The light from the living room window faded as clouds rolled over the sun. As the light dimmed, the old woman's face darkened. Deep black ruts formed beneath her eyes. Lines creased her forehead. She seemed to sag into the shadows.

"Here is my wish," I said in a trembling voice. I spoke slowly, carefully. I wanted to consider each word. I didn't want to slip up this time.

I didn't want to give her a chance to trick me.

"I am listening," she whispered, her face completely covered by shadow now. Except for her eyes, glowing as red as fire.

I cleared my throat. I took a deep breath.

"Here is my wish," I repeated carefully. "I wish for everything to return to normal. I want *everything* to be exactly the way it was — but —"

I hesitated.

Should I finish this part of it?

Yes! I told myself.

"I want everything to be the way it was — but I want Judith to think that I'm the greatest person who ever lived!"

"I will grant your third wish," she said, raising the glass ball high. "Your second wish will be canceled. Time will back up to this morning. Good-bye, Samantha."

"Good-bye," I said.

I was swallowed up by the radiating red glow. When it faded, Clarissa had vanished.

"Sam! Sam — rise and shine!"

My mother's voice floated up to my room from downstairs.

I sat straight up in bed, instantly awake. "Mom!" I cried happily.

I remembered everything. I remembered waking up in an empty house, in an empty world. And I remembered my third wish.

But time had gone back to this morning. I glanced at the clock. Seven. Mom was waking me up at the usual time.

"Mom," I leaped out of bed, ran downstairs in my nightshirt, and joyfully threw my arms around her, hugging her tight. "Mom!"

"Sam? Are you okay?" She stepped back, a startled expression on her face. "You running a fever?"

"Good morning!" I cried happily, hugging Punkin, who seemed just as startled. "Is Dad still home?" I was so eager to see him, too, to know that he was back.

"He left a few minutes ago," Mom said, still examining me suspiciously with her eyes.

"Oh, Mom!" I exclaimed. I couldn't conceal my happiness. I hugged her again.

"Whoa." I heard Ron enter the kitchen behind us.

I turned to see him staring at me, his eyes narrowed in disbelief behind his glasses. I ran over and hugged him, too.

"Mom — what did you put in her orange juice?" he demanded, struggling to back away from me. "Yuck! Let *go* of me!"

Mom shrugged. "Don't ever ask me to explain your sister," she replied dryly. She turned to the kitchen cabinets. "Go get dressed, Sam. You don't want to be late."

"What a beautiful morning!" I exclaimed.

"Yeah. Beautiful," Ron repeated, yawning. "You must have had some terrific dreams or something, Sam."

I laughed and hurried upstairs to get dressed.

I couldn't wait to get to school. I couldn't wait to see my friends, to see the halls filled once again with talking, laughing faces.

Pedaling my bike as hard as I could, I grinned every time a car passed. I loved seeing people again. I waved at Mrs. Miller across the street, bending to pick up her morning newspaper.

I didn't even mind it when the Carters' terrier came chasing after my bike, barking his high-pitched yips and nipping at my ankles.

"Good dog!" I cried gleefully.

Everything is normal, I told myself. Everything is wonderfully normal.

I opened the front door to school to the sound of crashing locker doors and shouting kids. "Great!" I cried aloud.

A sixth-grader came tearing around the corner and bumped right into me, practically knocking me over as I made my way to my locker. I didn't cry out angrily. I just smiled.

I was so *happy* to be back in school, back in my crowded, noisy school.

Unable to stop grinning, I unlocked my locker and pulled open the door. I called out a cheerful greeting to some friends across the hall.

I even said good morning to Mrs. Reynolds, our principal!

"Hey — Stork!" a seventh-grade boy called to me. He made a funny face, then disappeared around the corner.

I didn't care. I didn't care what anyone called me. The sound of so many voices was so wonderful!

As I started to take my coat off, I saw Judith and Anna arrive.

They were busy chatting, both talking at once. But Judith stopped when she saw me.

"Hi, Judith," I called warily. I wondered what Judith would be like now. Would she treat me any differently? Would she be nicer to me?

Would she remember how much she and I used to hate each other?

Would she be any different at all?

Judith gave Anna a little wave and came hurrying over to me. "Morning, Sam," she said, and smiled.

Then she pulled off her wool ski cap — and I gasped.

23

"Judith — your hair!" I cried in astonishment.

"Do you like it?" she asked, staring at me eagerly.

She had cut it shorter like mine and had tied a ponytail on the side — just like mine!

"I — I guess . . ." I stammered.

She breathed a sigh of relief and smiled at me. "Oh, I'm so glad you like it, Sam!" she cried gratefully. "It looks just like yours, doesn't it? Or did I cut it too short? Do you think it should be longer?" She studied my hair. "I think yours might be longer."

"No. No. It's . . . great, Judith," I told her, backing toward my locker.

"Of course, it's not as good as yours," Judith continued, staring at my ponytail. "My hair just isn't as pretty as yours. It isn't as fine, and the color is too dark."

I don't believe this! I thought.

"It looks good," I said softly.

I pulled my coat off and hung it in my locker. Then I bent to pick up my backpack.

"Let me carry that," Judith insisted. She grabbed it out of my hands. "Really. I don't mind, Sam."

I started to protest, but Anna interrupted. "What are you doing?" she asked Judith, flashing me a cold glance. "Let's get to class."

"You go without me," Judith replied. "I want to carry Sam's backpack for her."

"Huh?" Anna's mouth dropped open. "Are you totally losing it, Judith?" she demanded.

Judith ignored her question and turned back to me. "I love that T-shirt, Sam. It's ribbed, isn't it? Did you get it at the Gap? That's where I got mine. Look. I'm wearing one just like yours."

I goggled in surprise. Sure enough, Judith was wearing the same style T-shirt, only hers was gray and mine was pale blue.

"Judith — what's your problem?" Anna asked, applying the twentieth layer of bright orange lipstick on her lips. "And what did you do to your hair?" she cried, suddenly noticing the new style.

"Doesn't it look just like Sam's?" Judith asked her, flipping the ponytail with one hand.

Anna rolled her eyes. "Judith, have you gone psycho or something?"

"Give me a break, Anna," Judith replied. "I'd like to talk to Sam — okay?"

"Huh?" Anna knocked on Judith's head, as if knocking on a door. "Anyone home?"

"See you later, okay?" Judith said impatiently.

Anna sighed, then walked away angrily.

Judith turned back to me. "Can I ask you a favor?"

"Yeah. Sure," I replied. "What kind of favor?"

She hoisted my backpack over her left shoulder. Her own backpack hung on her right shoulder. "Would you help me work on my foul shot at practice this afternoon?"

I wasn't sure I had heard Judith correctly. I stared at her, my mouth hanging open.

"Would you?" she pleaded. "I'd really like to try shooting fouls your way. You know. Underhanded. I bet I'd have a lot more control shooting them underhanded, the way you do."

This was too much! *Too much!*

As I stared at Judith, I saw absolute *worship* in her eyes!

She was the best foul shooter on the team. And here she was, begging me to show her how to shoot the klutzy way I did it!

"Yeah. Okay. I'll try to help you," I told her.

"Oh, thank you, Sam!" she cried gratefully. "You're such a pal! And do you think I could borrow your social studies notes later? Mine are such a mess."

"Well . . ." I said thoughtfully. My notes were so bad, even I couldn't make them out.

"I'll copy them over and get them right back to you. Promise," Judith said breathlessly. I think the weight of two backpacks was starting to get to her.

"Okay. You can borrow them," I told her.

We started walking to class. Several kids stopped to stare at Judith, lugging two backpacks on her shoulders.

"Where did you get your Doc Martens?" she asked as we entered the room. "I want to get a pair just like yours."

What a laugh! I thought, very pleased with myself. *This is an absolute riot!*

The change in Judith was simply hilarious. It was all I could do not to burst out laughing.

Little did I know then that my laughter would quickly turn to horror.

It started to get really embarrassing. Judith wouldn't leave me alone.

She hung around me wherever I went. When I got up to sharpen my pencil, she followed me and sharpened hers.

My throat got dry during a spelling test, and I asked Lisa if I could run out to the water fountain to get a drink. As I was bending over the fountain, I turned and saw Judith right behind me. "My throat is dry like yours," she explained, faking a cough.

Later, during free reading, Lisa had to separate Judith and me because Judith wouldn't stop talking.

At lunch, I took my usual place across the table from Cory. I had just started telling him about Judith's new attitude — when she appeared at our table.

"Could you move down a seat?" she asked

the kid sitting next to me. "I want to sit next to Sam."

The kid moved, and Judith dropped her lunch tray onto the table and took her seat. "Would you like to trade lunches?" she asked me. "Yours looks so much better than mine."

I was holding a mushed-up tunafish sandwich. "This?" I asked, waving it. Half the tunafish fell out of the soggy bread.

"Yum!" Judith exclaimed. "Want my pizza, Sam? Here. Take it." She slid her tray in front of me. "You bring the best lunches. I wish my mom packed lunches like yours."

I could see Cory staring at me across the table, his eyes wide with disbelief.

I really couldn't believe it, either. All Judith wanted from the world was to be exactly like me!

A few tables away, near the wall, Anna sat by herself. She looked really glum. I saw her glance over to our table, frowning. Then she quickly lowered her eyes to her lunch.

After lunch, Judith followed me to my locker. She helped me pull out my books and notebooks and asked if she could carry my backpack.

At first, I thought this was all really funny. But then I started to get annoyed. And embarrassed.

I saw that kids were laughing at us. Two boys from my class followed us down the hall, snickering. I heard other kids talking about Judith and me in the hall. They stopped when Judith and I walked by, but I saw amused smirks on their faces.

She's making me look like a total jerk! I realized.

The whole school is laughing at us!

"Are you getting braces?" Judith asked me as we made our way back to the classroom. "Someone told me you were getting braces."

"Yeah. I'm getting them," I grumbled, rolling my eyes.

"Great!" Judith declared. "Then I want to get them, too!"

After school I hurried to the gym, expecting to have basketball practice. In all the excitement over the wishes, I had forgotten that we had an actual game that afternoon.

The girls' team from Edgemont Middle School was already on the floor, warming up by shooting layups. Most of their shots were dropping in. They were big, tough-looking girls. We had heard that they were a really good team — and they looked it.

I changed quickly and hurried out of the locker room. My teammates were huddled around Ellen for last-minute instructions. As I jogged over to them, I crossed my fingers on both hands and prayed that I wouldn't make too big a fool of myself in the game.

Judith grinned at me as I joined the huddle. Then she practically embarrassed me out of my Reeboks by shouting, "Here she is! Here comes our star!"

Anna and the others laughed, of course.

But then their smiles quickly faded when Judith interrupted Ellen to announce, "Before the game starts, I think we should name Sam team captain."

"You're joking!" Anna cried.

A few girls laughed. Ellen stared at me, bewildered.

"Our best player should be captain," Judith continued in all seriousness. "So it should be Sam, not me. All in favor, raise your hand."

Judith shot her hand up in the air, but no one else did.

"What's your problem?" Anna asked her nastily. "What are you trying to do, Judith — ruin our team?"

Judith and Anna got into an angry shouting match over that, and Ellen had to pull them apart.

Ellen stared at Judith as if she had lost her mind or something. Then she said, "Let's worry about who's captain later. Let's just go out and play a good game, okay?"

*   *   *

The game was a disaster.

Judith copied everything I did.

If I tried to dribble and tripped over my feet, Judith would dribble and trip. If I threw a bad pass that was intercepted by the other team, Judith would throw a bad pass.

When I missed an easy layup under the basket, Judith did the same thing, deliberately missing the next time she had the ball.

It was one flub after another — doubled because of Judith copying me!

And the whole time, she kept clapping and shouting, cheering me on. "Way to go, Sam! Nice try, Sam! You're the *best*, Sam!"

It was so obnoxious!

And I could see the girls on the Edgemont team snickering at us, and laughing out loud when Judith fell headfirst into the bleachers just because I had done it a few plays before.

Anna and the other players on my team weren't laughing. Their expressions were glum and angry.

"You're deliberately messing up!" Anna accused Judith about halfway through the game.

"I am *not*!" Judith replied shrilly.

"Why are you copying that clumsy ox?" I heard Anna demand.

Judith grabbed her and knocked her down, and they began wrestling angrily on the floor, screaming and tearing at each other furiously.

It took Ellen and the referee to stop the fight. Both girls were given a harsh lecture about sportsmanship and sent to the locker room.

Ellen made me sit down on the bench. I was glad. I really didn't feel like playing anymore.

As I watched the rest of the game, I couldn't concentrate on it at all. I kept thinking about my third and final wish, and how I'd blown it again.

To my dismay, I realized that having Judith worship me was much worse than having her hate me! At least when she hated me, she left me alone!

I had made three wishes, and each of them had turned into a nightmare. Now I was stuck with Judith following me around, hanging on my every word, constantly praising everything I did, fawning over me like a lovesick puppy — and, mainly, being an unbelievable pest!

I actually longed for the days when she had made fun of me in front of the whole class, when she had followed after me, calling, "Byrd, why don't you fly away! Why don't you fly away, Byrd!"

But what could I do? My three wishes were up.

Was I going to be stuck with Judith for the rest of my life?

We lost the game by fifteen or sixteen points. I didn't pay much attention to the score. I just wanted to get out of there.

But when I trudged into the locker room to change, Judith was waiting for me. She handed me a towel. "Good game!" she cried, slapping me a high five.

"Huh?" I could only gape at her.

"Can we study together after dinner?" she asked with pleading eyes. "Please? You could help me with my algebra. You're so much better at it than I am. You're a real genius when it comes to algebra."

Luckily, I had to go with my parents to visit my aunt after dinner. That gave me a good excuse not to study with Judith.

But what would be my excuse the next night? And the next, and the next?

My aunt wasn't feeling well, and the purpose of our visit was to cheer her up. I'm afraid I didn't do a very good job. I barely said a word.

I couldn't stop thinking about Judith.

What could I do about her? I could get angry and tell her to leave me alone. But I knew that wouldn't help. I had wished for her to think I was the greatest person who ever lived. Now Judith was under an enchantment, under the power of the Crystal Woman's spell.

Telling her to go away wouldn't discourage her in the least.

Could I just ignore her? That woudn't be easy

since she was constantly in my shadow, asking me a million questions, begging to wait on me like a servant.

What could I do? *What?*

I thought about it all the way home. Even my parents noticed I was distracted.

"What's the problem, Sam?" my mother demanded as we drove home.

"Oh, nothing," I lied. "Just thinking about schoolwork."

When we got home, there were four phone messages on the answering machine for me, all from Judith.

My mother stared at me, curious. "That's funny. I don't remember your being friends with her before," she said.

"Yeah. She's in my class," I told her. I didn't want to explain. I knew I *couldn't* explain.

I hurried up to my room. I was totally exhausted, from all the worrying, I guess. I got changed into a nightshirt, clicked off the light, and climbed into bed.

For a while, I lay staring up at the ceiling, watching shadows of the tree outside my window weave back and forth. I tried to clear my mind, tried to picture fluffy white sheep leaping over fluffy white clouds.

I was just drifting off to sleep when I heard the floorboards creak.

Opening my eyes wide, I saw a black shadow move against the darkness of my closet.

I uttered a choked cry as I realized that someone was in my room.

Before I could move, a hot, dry hand grabbed me by the arm.

I tried to scream, but the hand slid up over my mouth.

I — I'm going to choke! I thought, frozen in panic. *I can't breathe!*

"*Shh* — don't scream!" my attacker whispered.

The light clicked on.

The hand left my mouth.

"Judith!" I rasped, my voice catching in my throat.

She smiled at me, her green eyes flashing with excitement, and raised a finger to her lips. "*Shhhh.*"

"Judith — what are you *doing* here?" I managed to cry, finding my voice. My heart was still pounding so hard, I could barely breathe. "How did you get in?"

"Your back door was unlocked," she whispered. "I hid in the closet to wait for you. I guess I fell asleep for a little while."

"But why?" I demanded angrily. I pulled myself up and lowered my feet to the floor. "What do you want?"

Her smile faded. Her mouth formed a pout. "You said we could study together," she said in a little-girl voice. "So I waited for you, Sam."

This was the last straw. "Get out!" I cried.

I started to say more, but a knock on my door startled me into silence.

"Sam — are you okay?" my dad called in. "Are you talking to someone?"

"No. I'm fine, Dad," I said.

"You're not on the phone, are you?" he asked suspiciously. "You know you're not supposed to call people this late."

"No. I'm going to sleep now," I told him.

I waited till I heard his footsteps on the stairs. Then I turned back to Judith. "You have to go home," I whispered. "As soon as the coast is clear —"

"But why?" she demanded, hurt. "You said we'd study our algebra."

"I did not!" I cried. "Anyway, it's too late. You have to go home. Your parents must be going nuts worrying about you, Judith."

She shook her head. "I sneaked out. They think I'm asleep in bed." She smiled. "But that's so great of you to worry about my parents, Sam. You really are the most considerate girl I know."

Her stupid compliment made me even angrier. I was so furious, I wanted to tear her apart with my bare hands.

"I *love* your room," she gushed, glancing around quickly. "Did you pick out all the posters yourself?"

I sighed in total exasperation.

"Judith, I just want you to go home — now," I snarled slowly, one word at a time, so that maybe she would hear me.

"Can we study together tomorrow?" she pleaded. "I really need your help, Sam."

"Maybe," I replied. "But you can't sneak into my house anymore, and — "

"You're so smart," Judith gushed. "Where did you get that nightshirt? The stripes are terrific. I wish I had one like it."

Motioning for her to be silent, I crept out into the hall. All the lights had been turned off. My parents had gone to bed.

Tugging Judith by the hand, I led the way downstairs, tiptoeing silently, taking it one step at a time. Then I practically shoved her out the front door and swung it closed with a soft click behind her.

I stood in the dark entryway, panting hard, my mind racing.

What can I do? What can I do? What can I do?

It took me hours to get to sleep. And when I finally drifted off, I dreamed about Judith.

*   *   *

"You look tired, dear," my mom said at breakfast.

"I didn't sleep very well," I confessed.

When I headed out the front door to go to school, Judith was waiting for me by the driveway.

She smiled at me and waved cheerily. "I thought we could walk to school this morning," she chirped. "But if you want to ride your bike, I'll be happy to run alongside."

"No!" I shrieked. "No! Please — *no!*"

I totally lost it. I just couldn't stand it anymore.

I dropped my backpack and started to run. I didn't know where I was running. And I didn't care.

I just knew I had to run away from her.

"Sam — wait! Wait up!"

I turned to see her chasing after me. "No — please! Go away! Go *away!*" I screamed.

But I could see her pick up speed, her sneakers thudding against the sidewalk, starting to catch up.

I turned into someone's yard and ran behind a hedge, trying to lose her.

I didn't really know what I was doing. I had no plan, no destination. I just had to *run!*

I was running through backyards now, across driveways, behind garages.

And Judith followed, running at full speed, her short ponytail bobbing as she ran. "Sam — wait! Sam!" she called breathlessly.

Suddenly, I was running through woods, a thick tangle of trees and tall weeds. I weaved through them, first this way, then that, jumping over fallen branches, plunging through thick piles of dead brown leaves.

I've got to lose her! I told myself. *I've got to get away!*

But then I stumbled over an upraised tree root and fell, sprawling facedown on the carpet of dead leaves.

Typical klutz move.

And a second later, Judith was standing over me.

I glanced up from the ground and saw to my shock that it wasn't Judith.

Clarissa hovered over me, her red shawl tight around her shoulders, her black eyes staring intently.

"You!" I cried angrily, and started to scramble to my feet.

"You are unhappy," she said softly, frowning.

"Your wishes have ruined my life!" I cried, furiously brushing dead leaves off the front of my sweater.

"I don't want you to be unhappy," she replied. "I was trying to repay your kindness."

"I wish I'd never met you!" I cried angrily.

"Very well." She raised the round red crystal ball in one hand. As she raised it, her dark eyes began to glow, the same scarlet color as the crystal. "I will cancel your third wish. Make one final wish. Since you are so unhappy, I shall grant you one more."

I could hear the crunching of the leaves close behind me. Judith was catching up.

"I — I wish I'd never met you!" I cried to the Crystal Woman. "I wish *Judith* had met you instead of me!"

The crystal glowed brighter until the red light surrounded me in its glare.

When it faded, I was standing on the edge of the woods.

Whew! I thought. *What a relief! What a great break!*

I'm so lucky!

I could see Judith and Clarissa standing in the shade of a wide tree. They were huddled together, talking intently.

This is the perfect revenge! I told myself. *Now Judith will make a wish — and* her *life will be totally ruined!*

Chuckling to myself, I strained to hear what they were saying. I was dying to know what Judith would wish for.

I'm pretty sure I heard Judith say, "Byrd, why don't you fly away!"

But that didn't make any sense.

I was so happy! So deliriously happy!

I was free, totally free!

I suddenly felt so different. Lighter. Happier.

Let Judith have her wishes! I thought gleefully. *Let her see what it's like!*

Tilting my head, I saw a juicy brown earthworm

poke its head up from the ground. All of a sudden, I was feeling pretty hungry. I jabbed my head forward and caught the end of the worm. Then I ate it.

Very tasty.

I fluttered my wings, testing the wind.

Then I took off, flying low over the woods.

The cool breeze felt so refreshing against my feathers.

As I fluttered my wings harder, swooping higher into the sky, I glanced down and saw Judith. She was standing beside Clarissa.

Judith stared up at me from the ground, and I guess she got her first wish — because she had the *biggest* smile on her face!

BEHIND THE SCREAMS

BE CAREFUL WHAT YOU WISH FOR

CONTENTS

Bonus material
written and compiled by
Matthew D. Payne

About the Author

R.L. Stine's books are read all over the world. So far, his books have sold more than 300 million copies, making him one of the most popular children's authors in history. Besides Goosebumps, R.L. Stine has written the teen series Fear Street, the funny series Rotten School, as well as the Mostly Ghostly series, The Nightmare Room series, and the two-book thriller *Dangerous Girls*. R.L. Stine lives in New York with his wife, Jane, and Minnie, his King Charles spaniel. You can learn more about him at www.RLStine.com.

Q & A with R.L. Stine

If you were given three wishes, what would you wish for?

R.L. Stine (RLS): *That's really hard. The truth is my biggest wish came true: I wanted to be a writer—and I am. But if I do have two wishes left, I'd use one wish to travel back in time. And I'd use the second one to make sure I got back to the present!*

The main character in *Be Careful What You Wish For* is an enormous klutz on the basketball court. What's your most embarrassingly klutzy moment?

RLS: *It was just a couple of years ago. I was talking to a big crowd of important TV people and I told a story that I thought was really funny. But no one laughed. That got me so flustered that as I left the stage, I tripped and fell!*

Did you play any sports as a kid?

RLS: *No, I didn't play sports—unless you count Ping-Pong. But I loved to watch sports—especially football. In Ohio, everyone is crazy about football and I am still nuts about it. Go, Buckeyes!*

Your stories often take place in everyday schools and neighborhoods. How do you keep current on what kids are up to?

RLS: *My readers keep me up-to-date. Kids write to me and send me loads of messages at www.rlstine.com. Thanks, guys.*

There are Goosebumps books, websites, DVDs, and even a video game. Are there any new places where you'd like to see Goosebumps go?

RLS: *I love all the games and movies and DVDs—but most of all I like writing and having kids read my books. It's a real thrill for me that my books are read all over the world. You know what they call Goosebumps in France? Chair de Poule—that means chicken flesh. Cool, right?*

You've introduced readers to many fantastical fiends like the creatures in your latest book, Goosebumps Horrorland #7: *My Friends Call Me Monster*. Do you ever scare yourself with your creations?

RLS: *I never scare myself—and scary books and movies never scare me. The truth is, scary things make me* laugh! *I guess that means I'm a little weird, but it's true.*

To find out R.L. Stine's favorite photography subject, pick up the new collector's edition of **SAY CHEESE AND DIE!**

MAKE A WISH!

Don't have a crystal ball-carrying woman wandering around your neighborhood forest? Don't sweat! There are plenty of ways to make wishes without the aid of creepy old ladies. Here are a few:

THROW A COIN INTO A FOUNTAIN and make a wish! Here's the idea behind this wishing technique: The spirits who live in the water are more likely to grant your wish if you include a little payment. Seems like nobody does anything for free these days!

The next time you eat a turkey, **CRACK THE WISHBONE** with someone else. Whoever ends up with the larger piece will get to make a wish! Too busy to cook an entire turkey? No worries . . . fake wishbones are now available for mess-free wishing.

When you see a **ONE-EYED CAT**, spit on your thumb and then grind your thumb into the palm of your other hand while making a wish. Please make sure you saw a one-eyed cat first. We'd hate for you to go through all that spit-grinding trouble for no reason.

If you catch a **LADYBUG**, make a wish and then blow it *gently* out of the palm of your hand. If you blow too hard, you'll just make the ladybug angry and she probably won't grant your wish. And you'll be light-headed. GENTLE.

After you spot a **SHOOTING STAR**, make a wish. But be quick about it—some say finishing your wish before the shooting star disappears increases the chance it will come true.

On your next birthday, make a silent wish when you **BLOW OUT YOUR BIRTHDAY CANDLES**. In order for the wish to come true, make sure you don't say the wish out loud (to anyone!) and blow out *all* of the candles with one breath.

BLOWING AWAY AN EYELASH is a simple way to make a wish, if one happens to fall out. Don't PULL out eyelashes—only ones that fall out naturally have wishing power. Plus, that would really, really HURT!

The next time all the **NUMBERS ON YOUR DIGITAL CLOCK** match up (like 11:11), you can make a wish. After you make a wish, don't look at the numbers until they change, or your wish won't come true.

Fortune-Telling: Tools of the Trade

Nobody is sure where Clarissa, the Crystal Woman, came from. With her Crystal Ball and mysterious, wish-granting ways, she may very well be a fortune-teller! Of course, not everyone who has a crystal ball is a fortune-teller. And there are certainly many more ways to tell a fortune. Here are a few:

CRYSTAL BALLS are one of the top fortune-telling tools, since they're mighty handy for "scrying." **SCRYING** is the art of fortune-telling that involves staring into an object (usually clear or reflective) to catch images of the future.

Many objects can be used for scrying. Cultures all over the world use pools of water to scry: from the Zulus of Africa to Polynesians to remote villagers in Siberia. Think of *that* the next time you go swimming.

Other, less popular, scrying tools range from the convenient (fingernails) to the dirty (a pool of ink in the palm of the hand) to the disgusting (the liver of an animal). That last method sounds similar to a fortune-telling practice used by the ancient Greeks—**ARUSPICY**: An animal is sacrificed and its entrails are read to predict the future (ewww).

THROWING BONES involves throwing bones, shells, and other objects and then making predictions based on where and how all of the objects fall. This is a popular form of fortune-telling in Africa.

TAROT CARDS actually started as game cards in the fifteenth century. It wasn't until the 1700s that historians found records of fortune-tellers using the cards for readings.

PALMISTRY (reading the palm) is a fortune-telling technique used all over the world, from India (where the practice is thought to have started) to China and Europe. The different lines of the palm are read to predict the future. Take a look at your palm right now. See the line that runs from the spot between your thumb and pointing finger that runs all the way down to your wrist? That's your lifeline! Contrary to popular belief, it's not the length of the line that predicts how long you'll live.

HISTORY'S MOST FAMOUS FORTUNE-TELLER: The Oracle of Delphi altered the course of history with her predictions. The ancient Greeks consulted her on all important matters, especially those involving warfare.

FORTUNE COOKIES actually don't come from China—they first appeared in California in the early 1900s. Today, most of the fortunes found in fortune cookies are written by just two people!

Word Search!

Can you find all the words from Samantha's first wish? Refresh your memory by returning to page 31, then grab a pencil and circle each word as you find it. Make sure to look down, across, AND diagonally.

```
Q  B  A  Z  W  S  S  X  E  D  C
R  E  N  V  U  T  T  G  B  Y  H
N  U  J  M  F  R  E  I  K  O  L
P  M  Y  S  D  O  F  A  Q  W  E
G  H  J  M  W  N  B  X  M  P  L
Z  A  T  O  C  G  V  B  H  L  Y
V  W  E  R  D  E  F  G  A  A  J
P  I  L  O  K  S  M  B  I  Y  J
N  S  U  H  N  T  T  B  Y  E  G
V  T  F  C  R  E  D  C  X  R  E
S  Z  Q  A  K  T  C  M  Y  I  K
D  W  I  S  H  X  C  B  V  M  N
I  E  A  X  R  E  Y  T  W  V  A
I  B  D  V  A  E  P  S  H  X  Z
C  Z  W  I  H  T  D  F  R  E  O
```

Haunted Sports: Gaming Ghosts

Samantha's performance on the basketball court may have been scary, but much scarier things have happened in the world of sports.

Many athletes are afraid to grace the cover of *Sports Illustrated*, worried that they will be hit with the infamous *Sports Illustrated* Curse. Throughout the magazine's history, many teams and people who appeared on the cover suddenly had terrible things happen to them—a losing streak, an injury . . . EVEN DEATH.

Nationwide Arena in Columbus, OH, is thought to be haunted. It was built on the site of the former Ohio State Penitentiary, where several prisoners died in a terrible fire. True or not, many Columbus Blue Jackets hockey fans blame the bad performance of their team on paranormal activity!

In 1999, professional wrestler Owen Hart fell to his death while performing a stunt in Kansas City's Kemper Arena. It is believed that his ghost still haunts the arena, and there have been many reports of Hart, still in his wrestling costume, being seen in the rafters!

Baseball stadiums are ghost magnets, with examples of haunted fields found all across the country, from Angel Stadium in California to New York's Yankee Stadium. When human bones were found during construction of Frontier Field in Rochester, NY, strange things started happening. Paranormal experts were even brought in to investigate!

Finally, we tip our hats to the athletes who never stop playing! In 1996, pitcher Eddie Plank was heard practicing in his Gettysburg, PA, house . . . where he died 70 years before!

Don't Miss More Unexpected Endings in

#7 MY FRIENDS CALL ME MONSTER

Turn the page for a peek at the all-new, all-terrifying thrill ride from R.L. Stine.

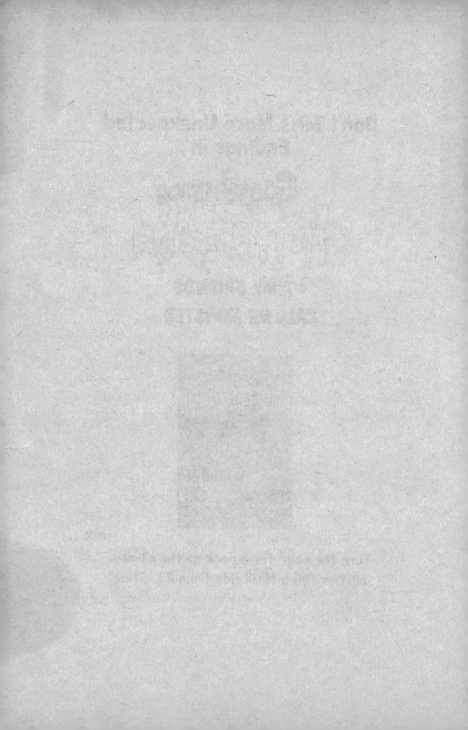

1

"Michael, this is crazy," my friend Daisy Edwards whispered. "We shouldn't be here."

"Too late," I whispered back. "We're already here."

Daisy was right. Sneaking into our teacher's house was probably a bad idea.

But there we were, the three of us — me, Daisy, and our friend DeWayne Walker — standing in Mrs. Hardesty's kitchen. My eyes darted around, trying to see in the dim light. All the shades were pulled.

"Weird. She keeps her house as dark as our classroom," DeWayne said.

The kitchen smelled of cinnamon. Mrs. Hardesty had a lot of snapshots on her fridge door. I glanced at them quickly. The faces all seemed blurry. An empty egg carton stood open on the sink.

I led the way into the front room. The shades were down there, too.

The couch and four chairs all matched. They were black leather. I saw knitting needles sticking out of a ball of wool on a table beside the couch. A tall wooden clock on the mantel ticked loudly.

"I'm not happy about this," Daisy whispered. "What if she comes home and finds us? We're *dead*!"

"No worries," I said. "She's still at school."

"Let's dump the cat and get *out* of here," DeWayne said. He raised the carrier in front of him. I could see the black cat's blue eyes peering out at me.

You're probably wondering why we sneaked into Mrs. Hardesty's house with a black cat. Well, our plan was simple.

Mrs. H is very superstitious. So . . . she comes home. She looks down and sees this black cat rubbing against her ankles . . . and it *totally* freaks her mind!

I wished I could be there when she went nuts. But I planned to be far, far away.

The cat pawed the front of the carrier and meowed. I think it wanted out.

"Monster, just open the carrier," DeWayne said. "Let it go, and we're *outta* here."

My friends call me Monster.

It's kind of a cool nickname. You see, I'm a big dude. I'm twelve, but I look like a high school guy. I'm pretty strong, too.

That's a *good* thing.

But I guess kids also call me Monster because of my temper. That's a *bad* thing.

My parents say I have a short fuse. That means I explode a lot. But, hey, I'm not angry *all* the time. Just when someone pushes my buttons.

Which is why my two friends and I were in Mrs. Hardesty's house. Our teacher had been pushing my buttons ever since she arrived at Adams Middle School.

"Let the cat out," DeWayne said, holding the carrier up to my face.

"Not here," I said. "Mrs. H will see it too soon. That's no fun."

"How about the basement?" Daisy said. "Mrs Hardesty opens the basement door, and there's a black cat at the bottom of the stairs, staring up at her. Can you picture it?"

"Awesome!" I said. I jabbed my finger into Daisy's forehead. "I like the way you think."

We searched the hall till we found the basement door. I pulled it open, and we stared down into the darkness. I fumbled for the light switch, and a bulb flashed on overhead.

I led the way down the creaky wooden steps. The cat meowed again. "Be patient," I said. "You'll have a nice, new basement to explore. And Mrs. H will take good care of you."

We stepped into a short hallway. The air grew cold and damp. The basement was divided into two rooms. Both doors were shut.

DeWayne set the carrier down on the floor. He bent to open its door.

That's when we heard the sound. A heavy *thump*. From one of the rooms.

We all froze. DeWayne's hands shot up, away from the carrier. He stared at me, his mouth open. Daisy took a step back.

I heard a groan. Another *thump*.

My heart did a flip-flop in my chest. "There's someone down here!" I whispered.

We didn't say another word. DeWayne grabbed the carrier by the handle, we spun away from the doors, and took off.

We scrambled up the stairs. Our sneakers thudded loudly all the way up.

I was nearly at the top when I heard a metal *chiiing*. Something hit a stair and bounced down.

"Something fell out of my pocket!" I cried.

Was it my cell phone?

I couldn't go back for it. We had to get out of there.

Someone — or some*thing* — was coming after us!

TWO WEEKS EARLIER

"How many of you have heard of the Loch Ness Monster?" Mrs. Hardesty asked. Several hands went up.

"Here she goes again," I whispered to DeWayne. He sat beside me in class.

DeWayne rolled his eyes. "Always monsters."

"The other sixth-grade class is doing the Civil War," I said. "All we talk about is monsters. How weird is that?"

DeWayne laughed. He's a lanky, good-looking dude. He wears low-riding, baggy jeans and long T-shirts with hip-hop singers across the front. He has big brown eyes and keeps his black hair shaved close to his head.

He's a good guy, except his laugh is too loud, which gets me in trouble a lot.

I suddenly realized Mrs. Hardesty had her

beady little black eagle eyes on me. "Is something funny, Michael?" she asked.

I shrugged.

"Would you like to share it with the whole class?"

I shrugged again. "Whatever."

I should've just said *sorry* or something. Why do I always look for trouble with her?

Maybe because she's always on my case?

She stared at me with that cold expression, her face frozen like a statue.

Mrs. Hardesty looks a lot like a bird, with tiny round eyes pushed up against a long beaky nose. She has short, feathery, white-blond hair that puffs up around her pale narrow face.

"Would you care to tell the class what *you* think the Loch Ness Monster looks like, Michael?"

"Well . . . it looks a lot like DeWayne, except it's prettier."

That got everyone laughing, except for Mrs. Hardesty. She wrinkled her nose and made that sniffing sound she always makes when she's unhappy about something.

She held up a large photograph. "This is a photo of the Loch Ness Monster," she said. She moved it from side to side, but it was really hard to see in the dim light.

She always keeps it dark in the room. Kids are always stumbling over their backpacks. When we take tests, we have to hold the paper up close to our faces to read it.

It was a bright, sunny day outside, but the shades were down and the ceiling lights were dim as usual.

"As you can see, the monster looks a lot like a dinosaur," Mrs. Hardesty continued. "A lot of people claim this photo is a fake. People don't want to believe in monsters."

I reached into my jeans pocket and pulled out my silver dog whistle.

"But hundreds of people visit the lake in Scotland every year," Mrs. H said. "They want to see the monster for themselves."

Kids gasped in surprise as one of the window shades shot up with a loud *snap*. Sunlight poured into the room.

Mrs. Hardesty shielded her eyes. She edged sideways to the window and tugged the shade back down. The room grew dark again.

Mrs. Hardesty picked up her lucky rabbit's foot from the desk. She always squeezes it in her hand when she gets tense. Which means she squeezes it a *lot*!

"Many other water monsters have been spotted over the centuries," she said. "In ancient times, sailors believed in sea serpents. And —"

SNAP.

The same window shade zipped back up to the top.

Mrs. H gasped and dove to the window. She tugged it down and held it there for a few seconds. Then she returned to the front of her desk, rolling the rabbit's foot in her hand.

SNAP.

The shade flipped back up. Everyone laughed. Sunlight poured over the front of the room.

I hid the dog whistle under my desk. She hadn't seen me blow it. She had no idea what a mechanical genius Michael Munroe is.

Yeah, I'm real good with tech stuff. People don't expect it, because I'm Monster, the big hulk of a dude who is always getting into trouble.

But I've got a lot of skill with computers and all kinds of tech stuff.

Before class, I rigged the window shade. I put a tiny receiver on it. The dog whistle sent high-pitched sound waves to the receiver. Sound waves that humans can't hear. And the sound made the window shade go flying up.

SNAP.

I did it again. Just to upset Mrs. H and get everyone laughing. Then I hid the whistle behind my textbook.

Mrs. Hardesty scratched her head. "Why does that shade keep going up?" she asked.

"Maybe an *evil spirit* is doing it!" DeWayne said.

He knew I was doing it. But he liked to torture her, too. "*Owooooo*." He made a nice ghost howl.

Mrs. Hardesty's mouth dropped open. She didn't think it was funny. She was squeezing that lucky rabbit's foot *flat*!

"One should never joke about evil spirits," she said. Her voice trembled.

She kept a jar of black powder on her desk. She reached into the jar, pulled out a handful, and tossed it over her shoulder.

Is she the weirdest teacher on earth or *what*?

We're always trying to figure out what the black powder is. Daisy thinks it's ground-up bat wings. DeWayne says it's powdered eye of newt. He learned about eye of newt in one of the scary books he's always reading.

Mrs. Hardesty tugged the window shade down and examined it carefully. I hoped she wouldn't spot the little receiver I'd planted there.

She returned to the front of the class. I raised my dog whistle and prepared to blow it again.

OOPS.

The whistle slipped out of my hand. I made a wild grab for it. But it bounced off my desk, hit the floor, and rolled halfway to Mrs. Hardesty.

Did she see it?

Yes.

She squinted at it, then raised her eyes to me. "Uh . . . am I in trouble?" I asked.

3

Yes, I was in trouble. She made me come back to class after school.

Outside, rain clouds covered the sky. That made the classroom even darker than before.

Mrs. Hardesty had two tall white candles flickering on her desk. She was leaning over them, whispering to herself, when I dragged myself in.

"Mrs. Hardesty, I'm sorry about the whistle thing," I said. "But I can't stay after school."

She kept whispering for a long while, her eyes shut. The candle smoke floated over her face, but she didn't seem to mind it.

Finally, she looked up at me. Her skin appeared gray and powdery in the candlelight. "Of course you will stay, Michael."

"No. Really," I said. "I can't. I'll miss wrestling practice."

Monster Munroe is the captain of the wrestling team. Who else?

"Sit down, Michael," Mrs. H said. She pointed to a chair. "I want you to wrestle with your thoughts."

I let out a groan. "I can't go to practice?"

She reached into her jar and tossed a little black powder over her shoulder. "Sit down," she said.

I sat down. I threw my backpack angrily to the floor. I muttered some bad words under my breath.

I had that burning feeling in my chest. The feeling I get when someone is making me really mad.

Mrs. Hardesty blew out the candles. She seemed to inhale the smoke. "Michael, do you think it's smart to make a fool of your teacher?" she asked.

"I really didn't have to try!" I blurted out.

OOPS. I did it again. Why can't I ever shut my trap?

I heard kids burst out laughing in the hall. I knew it was Daisy and DeWayne.

Mrs. Hardesty leaped up from behind her desk. She strode to the classroom door and dragged my two friends in.

DeWayne plopped down next to me, shaking his head.

Daisy didn't look too happy, either. She never gets in trouble. She has this cute, innocent look. Curly carrot-colored hair, lots of freckles, and dimples in her cheeks even when she isn't smiling. So everyone thinks she's totally sweet and adorable.

Of course, I know better. I know she has a wicked-cold sense of humor. She could be a big problem child like me — if she put her mind to it.

"We didn't do anything," Daisy told Mrs. Hardesty. "Why do we have to stay?"

The teacher waved for Daisy to sit down. Then she frowned at us one by one.

"You three need an attitude change," she said. She rubbed her pointed chin. "I think I know what will help."

"Me, too," I said. "Wrestling practice will help me. It'll change my attitude. Really."

DeWayne grinned at Mrs. Hardesty. "I got an A in Attitude last semester," he said. "You can check it out."

Mrs. Hardesty rolled her eyes. "We don't grade for attitude," she muttered.

DeWayne squinted at her. "You sure?"

He was goofing on her. But she never got a joke.

"I know what will help you," Mrs. H repeated. "Some honest work."

All three of us groaned.

"I'll give you a choice," she said. "You can stay two hours after school every day for a week."

We groaned again, louder.

"Or you can do some community service," Mrs. H said.

We stared blankly at her. I had a sudden urge to take out my dog whistle and make the shade fly up again.

"I have a project that's perfect for you three," Mrs. Hardesty said. "It's in the lot right by my house. You can come on Saturday."

"I can't," I said. "My dad is taking me to the big computer tech show. I —"

"I can't," Daisy said. "I have my tennis lesson, and —"

"Saturday," Mrs. Hardesty insisted. "No excuses."

The three of us started complaining to each other.

"Listen up," Mrs. Hardesty said. "This is important. Be sure to wear work clothes on Saturday. And you'd better bring nose plugs."

Huh? *Nose plugs?*

What did she want us to *do* on Saturday?

Catch the
MOST WANTED
Goosebumps® villains
UNDEAD OR ALIVE!

scholastic.com/goosebumps

Available in print
and eBook editions

GBMW9

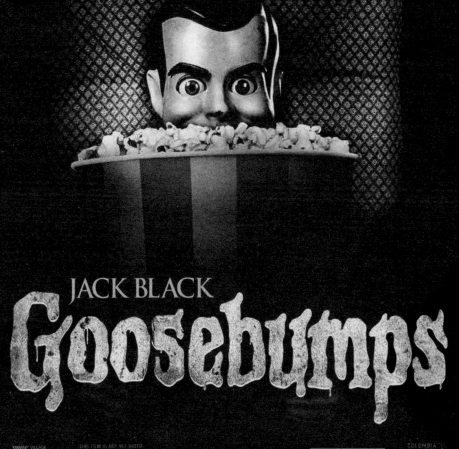